KHLC
KT-479-519
28 APR 2011
BEANEY
11 NOV 2011
28 NOV 2011
09/09/13

CHARTER MARK

Kent
County
Council

C155285113

More Than a Millionaire

EMILIE ROSE

First published in Great Britain 2010
Large Print edition 2010
Harlequin Mills & Boon Limited,
Eton House, 18-24 Paradise Road,
Richmond, Surrey TW9 1SR

ISBN: 978 0 263 22152 7

Harlequin Mills & Boon policy is to use papers that are natural, renewable and recyclable products and made from wood grown in sustainable forests. The logging and manufacturing process conform to the legal environmental regulations of the country of origin.

Printed and bound in Great Britain
by CPI Antony Rowe, Chippenham, Wiltshire

EMILIE ROSE

Bestselling Desire author and RITA® Award finalist Emilie Rose lives in her native North Carolina with her four sons and two adopted mutts. Writing is her third (and hopefully her last) career. She's managed a medical office and run a home day care, neither of which offers half as much satisfaction as plotting happy endings. Her hobbies include gardening and cooking (especially cheesecake). Her favourite TV shows include *Grey's Anatomy, ER, CSI, Dancing with the Stars, American Idol* and Discovery Channel's Medical programs. Emilie's a rabid country music fan because she can find an entire book in almost any song.

Letters can be mailed to:
Emilie Rose
PO Box 20145
Raleigh, NC 27619
USA

Email: EmilieRoseC@aol.com

JBR you light up the room (and me)
with nothing more than a smile.

No matter what happens,
my time with you has truly been
a gift I will never regret.

One

"Define *unfortunate incident,*" Ryan Patrick ordered the director of the Lakeview Fertility Clinic from the visitor's side of the ornate walnut desk.

The director's leather chair creaked, revealing each nervous shift of the man's body. "One of our trainees neglected to cross-reference the lot number on your sample. He only checked the names and those were reversed. I want to assure you, Mr. Patrick, this is an unusual circumstance. We have many checks and balances in place to—"

"What does this mean? To me. Specifically," Ryan cut in impatiently. He unclenched his fingers from the arms of the chair, but it was hard to relax when the man in front of him looked like he was about to have a heart attack at any second.

The director inhaled a long, deep breath. "Your contribution was given to the wrong woman."

Ryan's abdominal muscles tensed. That would only be a problem if—

"Her pregnancy was confirmed two weeks ago," the director added.

Problem. One that jeopardized Ryan's goal of proving to his father that he'd settled down and was ready to take over the reins of the Patrick architectural dynasty. But Ryan was a master troubleshooter. He wouldn't have climbed this far up the ladder of success if he'd thrown in the towel at every obstacle.

Too bad his father couldn't see that.

"Two weeks ago? Why am I just now being informed? And what about my surrogate, the woman I hired?"

"We discovered the situation yesterday when she came in for her appointment. She wasn't inseminated since at your insistence we only had the one vial."

They'd only had one vial because with the reputation of this place he'd expected them to get it right the first time.

"And you're certain this other woman is pregnant with *my* child?"

"Yes, sir."

Ryan tamped down his frustration. Once he'd decided to take the surrogate route he'd spent months interviewing to find the right candidate—one with looks, brains and good genetics. One who wouldn't get emotionally attached to the baby she hosted in her womb for nine months and change her mind about handing over his child.

And now the wrong woman was carrying his baby.

"Who is she?"

"I'm not at liberty to release that information, sir."

Ryan exploded to his feet. "You're not at liberty to tell me who's carrying *my* child?"

"Yes. Confidentiality—"

Ryan intended to get the information one way

or the other. He braced his fists on the desk and leaned forward.

"Don't make me bring a platoon of lawyers in here. Not only will that be financially costly for you, the negative publicity will knock you right off the list of top fertility clinics in the country. This is my kid, and I have the right to know who and where its mother is and whether she's qualified for the job. I want *everything* you have on her."

The director's face flushed dark red. "Mr. Patrick, I'm sure you understand the privacy of Lakeview's business—"

"I want her name and contact information now. Otherwise my legal team will be all over you like a bad rash before lunch."

The man stiffened and swallowed then fumbled with a folder on his desk. "I'm sure that won't be necessary. Ms. High—our other client seems like a reasonable, understanding woman. Once I explain the situation to her—"

"I'll handle it. You've screwed up enough. You can cover up your mistake with words like *incident, circumstance* and *situation,* but the truth is you've committed malpractice and negligence."

Sweat beaded beneath the man's receding hairline. Ryan eyed him without blinking. Once the man paled, Ryan knew he'd get what he wanted without the aggravation of lawyers. Good. He did not want his father to catch wind of this disaster.

"*Ahem.* I'll get you the information, sir."

Ryan settled back in the chair when the director hustled out. Next on his agenda: find this woman and convince her to give him his baby—the way the surrogate he'd chosen had agreed to.

She would be the best aunt her baby could have.

And it would be enough. It had to be.

Nicole Hightower rubbed one hand over her unsettled stomach and reached for a cracker with the other. She was finally going to have Patrick's baby.

And Beth's.

Her fingers spasmed around the stylus of her PDA at the reminder that her dream wasn't going exactly as she'd once planned.

She shoved the bland whole-wheat cracker into her mouth and tried to focus on the calendar in front of her. She needed to schedule the client's pilot, crew and plane maintenance for the next three months. She usually loved keeping her customers happy and their travel stress-free, but today her private life kept distracting her from the workload on her desk.

Relinquishing her baby would be hard, but she could handle it because she would be not only a godmother, but also a hands-on aunt. Her sister had promised, and Beth kept her promises. Nicole had always been able to count on her big sister—even at the times when she hadn't been able to count on their parents. Carrying a child for Beth was the least Nicole could do.

And since her sister would continue to work at Hightower Aviation Management and bring the baby to work every day, Nicole looked forward to going down the hall to the on-site day care and visiting her—*Beth's*—baby during lunch. Even from her desk she'd be able to observe her b—niece or nephew. She clicked on an icon on her computer screen and a live feed from the company nursery filled her monitor. The caregivers bustled around, tending to the adorable children of HAMC's employees.

The intercom buzzed jarring her from her tangled thoughts. She quickly broke the nursery link. "Yes?"

"There's a Ryan Patrick here to see you."

Nicole smiled over her assistant's mistake. "You mean Patrick Ryan."

"No, I don't. I'm not talking about your brother-in-law," Lea whispered. "I'm talking about the gorgeous black-haired, blue-eyed, towering hunk of manhood standing in the reception area. His business card says he's the VP at Patrick Architectural Designs. That's one of Knoxville's most prestigious firms, in case you didn't know. Are we expanding again?"

"As far as I know Hightower Aviation isn't planning to build any new structures." But then her oldest brother, Trent, the CEO, didn't tell her everything. As the youngest Hightower offspring until recently, Nicole was often kept out of the loop.

She double-checked her calendar to make sure she hadn't forgotten an appointment and found no one scheduled for another hour. Then, because she didn't like to go into a meeting unprepared, she typed Patrick Architectural Designs into her Internet search engine. A series of links popped up on her screen. She chose the one that looked the most useful, clicked and scanned the Web page. There were no pictures of the man in question, only of buildings designed by his company and a brief company history. Impressive. They'd been around awhile.

"Patrick Architectural is a commercial firm with projects across the continent," she said into the intercom. "Do you think Mr. Patrick might be a potential client?"

Although normally new clients came to her through the sales department *after* they'd purchased, leased or bought shares in an aircraft.

His name was an interesting coincidence, though.

"I prefer my fantasy to your logic," Lea quipped.

"You always have, Lea. Bring him back."

"Yes, ma'am."

Nicole brushed the crumbs from her silk blouse and into the trash can then slid the sleeve of crackers into her drawer. She rose just as Lea tapped on her door and pushed it open.

The man striding into her office like he owned the place was everything her assistant had said and more. Lea hadn't mentioned her visitor's short hair had a curl that he couldn't quite subdue or that his shoulders filled out his navy suit jacket like a tailor's dream above a flat stomach, lean hips and long legs. And his eyes weren't just blue; they were an amazingly intense shade of cobalt. Those eyes assessed her now as he would a Learjet he was considering purchasing.

Nicole fought the urge to check her neckline and the corners of her mouth for more crumbs.

"Nicole Hightower?"

Even his voice had a deep and slightly rough sexual fantasy quality. Not that she ever fantasized about clients. That would be totally unprofessional.

And too much like her mother.

She walked around the corner of her desk and extended her arm. "Yes. How can I help you, Mr. Patrick?"

His handshake was warm and firm and electrified.

Giving up caffeine must be having unforeseen side effects on her system. Why else would she experience a faux espresso buzz on contact? She broke the connection as quickly as courtesy allowed.

His intense gaze shifted to Lea and conveyed something that made the redhead snap to attention. "I'll just...go now."

Surprised, Nicole watched her usually unflappable assistant hustle out the door and close it behind her.

Nicole reappraised the man in front of her. Besides tall, dark and gorgeous, he had some kind of magical talent. She'd have to figure out what trick he'd used to make Lea leave without saying a word.

Lea wasn't only an employee. She was also a friend and sometimes the line between friend and supervisor blurred—like when Lea had voiced her vehement disapproval of Nicole's decision to become a surrogate for her sister and brother-in-law. But that was because Lea knew how Nicole felt about her sister's husband. They'd been college roommates when Nicole had fallen head over heels in love with Patrick. And Lea had been there to help pick up the pieces after Patrick had eloped with Nicole's sister Beth.

Lea was convinced that the entire "baby debacle," as she referred to it, was going to blow up in Nicole's face now that she was pregnant.

"Please sit down, Mr. Patrick, and tell me what I can do for you today."

Nicole felt his gaze on her the entire way around her desk as she returned to her seat. Pregnancy had made her breasts larger. She hoped it hadn't done the same to her behind. Not that she cared what he thought of her butt.

After she sank into her seat he lowered himself into the chair across from her desk. The old-fashioned courtesy surprised her. Fewer and fewer men practiced it these days—especially among the megarich she dealt with through work.

"Congratulations on your pregnancy."

His words stunned her. She hadn't told anyone except Beth, Patrick and Lea. The parents-to-be had the right to know, and Lea had caught Nicole heaving a couple of times and guessed. The rest of their friends and family would find out Saturday when Beth and Patrick made the official announcement at the family's Labor Day picnic. Nicole suspected most people who knew her would be a little freaked out by her decision.

"Thank you. What brings you to Hightower Aviation today?"

"You're carrying my child."

His statement knocked her back in her chair. She must have misheard.

"Excuse me?" The words sounded more like a wheeze, but that was because she couldn't seem to make her lungs work.

"The fertility clinic made a mistake and inseminated you with my sperm instead of your intended donor's."

Head reeling, she grasped the edge of her desk. "That's not possible."

Her visitor reached into his suit coat, extracted an envelope and extended it toward her. When she didn't—couldn't—take it from him he tossed it on her blotter. It slid across the smooth surface and stopped within easy reach. She eyed it like she would a big, hairy, jumping spider.

"The clinic director has written a letter explaining the situation. In summation, my name is Ryan Patrick. Your intended donor's name is Patrick Ryan. The lot numbers weren't checked and you were given the wrong sperm because some moron neglected to notice a comma."

Horror raced through her, making her heart pound and her extremities tingle. "No. You're wrong."

He had to be.

"Read it."

She stared at the envelope. Afraid to open it. Afraid not to. But she couldn't prove him wrong if she didn't open the thing. Her hands shook as she reached for it.

The tearing of the seal and the rustle of paper as she unfolded the page sounded unnaturally loud even above the pounding of her pulse in her ears. The letter bore the Lakeview logo at the top and the director's signature on the bottom. She forced herself to read through the document.

Words jumped out at her. *Unfortunate error… Donor mix-up… Apologize profusely…* The alarm in her chest and her brain expanded with each line, making it difficult to breathe and think. She read the letter a second time, but the bad news didn't get any better, and she hadn't misinterpreted.

Unless this letter was a hideously tasteless joke, she was carrying Ryan Patrick's baby. Not Patrick Ryan's, the man she had loved since her junior year of college. The man who'd married her sister.

Please, God, let this be a joke.

"This is not funny."

Her visitor didn't crack a smile. "Medical malpractice usually isn't."

She had hoped her sister had developed a sudden sick sense of humor. His stoic expression said otherwise. Pressing a hand over her churning stomach, she dropped the page. "There must be some mistake."

"Yes. Lakeview Fertility Clinic made it. You're carrying my child as a result."

"That can't be right."

"I wish that were true."

She stared at the letter while her overloaded mind struggled to process the information and the possible repercussions. For herself. For Beth and Patrick. For the man in front of her. But it was too much to take in.

What now? What if the baby really wasn't Patrick's?

She struggled to find her professional demeanor, and the best way to do that was to focus on his problem instead of hers. "I'm sorry. This must be very difficult for you and your wife."

"There is no wife."

"Girlfriend, then."

"No girlfriend, either."

That confused her completely. "I'm afraid I'm not following."

"I'll be a single parent."

"That's not unusual for a woman, but isn't it a little out of the norm for a man? Couldn't you just get married?"

"I've been married, and I don't ever intend to do so again."

There had to be a story behind that bitter tone. But she didn't care to hear it at the moment. She had enough of a mess on her hands. *If* his story was true. She sincerely hoped he was deranged. A psycho in her office would be much easier to handle than the situation described in the letter. One call to security would fix everything. But this…

He extracted a second envelope and placed it in front of her. "I'm prepared to offer you the same financial and medical support I offered the surrogate I'd hired."

Taken aback, she blinked. "You hired a surrogate?"

Why would a guy who looked like him need to pay someone to have his baby? Women should be lining up around the block and begging for the privilege.

"A well-qualified, carefully screened surrogate."

She bristled at his implication that she might be less than qualified to carry his child. For the second time this morning she forced herself to read something she didn't want to and picked up the contract.

Shocked, she looked up from the document that had her name typed in all the appropriate places. "You want to *buy* my baby?"

Duh. That's what surrogacy is, Nicole. But seeing it in black and white rattled her.

"It's a service contract. You provide a product

and a service. I pay you for your time and the use of your body," he replied as coolly as if they were haggling over the price of an airplane.

A product? Revulsion slammed her chest a split second before an unexpected surge of possessiveness swelled within her. She wrapped her arms around her middle. Until now she'd been ready to hand over her baby to Beth and Patrick. With dignity. Without a fight. But she'd be damned if she'd *sell* it to this stranger.

"You are out of your mind, Mr. Patrick."

"It's my child."

"It's mine, too. My egg. My body. My time."

"My terms are quite generous."

She tossed the document back at him. He made no effort to catch it. The pages fluttered to the desk. "I don't care about your terms. Go back to your surrogate."

"And forget I've already fathered one child?"

"Yes. You have no emotional investment here and no financial obligation. You can have another baby much easier than I can. I will carry this child for nine months. Your contribution only took seconds."

"You're only eight weeks pregnant. You haven't had time to bond."

Her mouth dropped open. She snapped it closed. "Spoken like a man who doesn't have a clue. You have no idea what you're talking about."

She'd begun bonding from the first moment she'd noticed her taste buds had gone crazy—just days after conception and even before the positive pregnancy test. She remembered the exact moment she'd realized she was pregnant with Patrick's baby.

According to *him* it wasn't Patrick's baby.

He might be wrong. Please, please let him be wrong.

"I'm sorry. I'm not going to believe your story without proof."

"You have it." He indicated the letter by dipping his chin.

"This is not enough." She'd go through the clinic's records personally, if need be. And if that didn't work…there was always DNA testing. How soon could that be done? And was it safe for the baby? She jotted down the questions to ask her doctor.

Her visitor's jawline hardened. "You're only twenty-eight. You have time to have other children."

Unlikely, since her heart was already taken. "You're not exactly ancient."

"I'm thirty-five."

"Women have a shorter window of opportunity for reproducing than men. You can keep fathering children for another fifty years."

His lips thinned in irritation. "I want a child now, and I'm not walking away and leaving the door open for you to sue me for child support."

The jerk's personality did not improve with exposure. Usually she could find something to like about even the most difficult person. Not so here. Other than his physical packaging which was prime.

She took a deep breath and reminded herself that any problem could be solved with patience, politeness and perseverance. Her three *P*'s never let her down.

"I would never do that, Mr. Patrick. I don't want or expect anything from you."

His eyebrows lowered. "You expect me to take the word of a stranger?"

She was too busy reeling over the possibility that she might be carrying a stranger's baby to care what he thought.

"I'm not interested in your money, and I'm willing to have my attorney draft a document stating that fact and relieving you of all responsibility."

"That would be useless. You'd have eighteen years to change your mind."

She wanted to smack him. "Mr. Patrick, I couldn't give you this child even if I wanted to—which I don't."

She pressed her fingertips to her stomach and gathered the words that had become her mantra since she'd committed to this plan. "This baby is not mine. I'm carrying it for my sister and brother-in-law."

Who might not want the baby if it wasn't Patrick's.

Oh my God.

Panic tightened her chest. A cold sweat seeped through her pores. What was she going to do? She certainly wasn't handing her baby to this knuckle-dragging Neanderthal who acted as if giving up her child would be as easy as giving a panhandler the change from her pocket.

"You're acting as a surrogate for someone else?"

His clipped words interrupted her chaotic thoughts. "Yes. Patrick Ryan is my brother-in-law."

"How much is he paying you?"

Appalled, she reared back. "Nothing. This is a gift."

"I'm offering a hundred thousand, plus expenses. You're going to give up the kid. Why not to me? You can have his kid next year."

His cavalier attitude winded her. "I'm not a broodmare."

She'd geared herself up to do this once. She didn't think she could handle giving a baby away a second time.

"I'll make it worth your while."

"No, thank you. I gave my word." For once she wanted to come through for Beth instead of having Beth make all the sacrifices for her. She owed her sister a huge debt.

And she wanted to give Patrick something Beth couldn't.

Not nice, Nicole.

"Tell her you changed your mind. If the egg is yours, then the child is in no way hers or her husband's."

She flinched and wished he'd quit reminding her of that.

Adrenaline surged through her veins. If the baby wasn't Patrick's then it was *hers.*

Hers and the Neanderthal's.

"I signed a contract," she said more to herself than to him. So where did that leave her? Was the contract even valid if the baby wasn't Patrick's?

"Contracts can be broken."

She needed to talk to her lawyer before tackling the legalities. "You don't understand. I will be this child's aunt. I'll see it almost every day. I'll get to watch him or her grow up and be a part of its life. I'll still be family."

She hated the anxiety sharpening her voice. The idea had sounded so much better before her pregnancy had been confirmed. "Go back to your surrogate."

"You're carrying my firstborn and firstborn Patricks have taken over the family firm for three generations."

"What if my child doesn't want to be an architect?"

One dark eyebrow hiked. "Why wouldn't he?"

"Because I don't have an artistic bone in my body and he or *she* might take after me."

"Or he might take after me and be damned good at it. Don't turn this into a legal battle, Ms. Hightower."

His threat was clear. The muscles of her spine went rigid and her heart thumped even harder. Her arms tightened protectively around her middle. They'd done that a lot since he'd walked in. "This is my baby."

"Is it, if you've already signed away your rights? As the child's biological father I probably have more rights to it than you do."

Fear slithered down her spine. She was very afraid that what he said might be true, but she wasn't giving up without a fight. She glared at him, silently telling him to bring it on. The stiffening of his features told her he'd received her message loud and clear. He stood and towered over her.

She rose to meet him at his level, but still had to tilt her head back. How tall was he, anyway? Well over six feet.

"This discussion is over, Mr. Patrick, until I talk to my attorney."

"Do that. Mine will be calling you. But be warned, Ms. Hightower, I always get what I want, and I will be a father to my child. Make it easy on yourself, accept that and don't prolong this."

He turned on his heel, flung open her door and stalked out of her office, sucking all the oxygen with him as he went.

Sapped of strength, but conversely filled with an energizing surplus of adrenaline, Nicole sank into her chair. She had to do something to stop him. Because if Ryan Patrick had his way she would be giving up far more than the right to mother her baby. She might never see her child again. And that was not going to happen.

Two

Apparently it didn't matter which side of the desk Nicole sat on. Today was her day to receive bad news.

She stared in dismay at the woman in front of her. "You're saying he's correct. Ryan Patrick has more right to my baby than I do?"

While her attorney's smile and brown eyes were sympathetic, they didn't offer much encouragement. "I'm sorry, Nicole. The clinic confirmed his story. There was a mix-up. Biologically, this is his child unless DNA testing proves otherwise."

"But my doctor said I couldn't do prenatal DNA testing without significant risk to the baby. So that's out of the question." Nicole had called her in a panic the minute Ryan Patrick left her office. "I don't think I can stand seven more months of uncertainty."

"I understand. And it really isn't necessary since the lot number of Ryan Patrick's…contribution was found written on your record. Too bad the technician didn't double-check it beforehand."

She was carrying a stranger's baby.

Not Patrick's.

Disappointment and helpless frustration filled her with an antsy urge to climb out of her skin. "Is the contract even valid since the baby isn't Patrick's?"

"The wording states you're providing them with a child, and that you have no intention of claiming that child. It doesn't specify paternity. The agreement is pretty ironclad. They used all the right phrases to protect themselves in case you changed your mind, and since we didn't think that would be an issue, I didn't strike or amend the clause."

A heavy weight settled on Nicole's chest. "I don't want Ryan Patrick to get custody. If he does, I may never see my baby again. At least Beth promised me I could be a hands-on aunt."

"But you didn't get that promise in writing, so it wouldn't hold up in court. I wish I could say the chances of Mr. Patrick winning at least partial custody were slim, but they're not.

"This isn't your fight, Nicole, unless you elect to try and revoke your surrogacy contract which I can tell you will be a tough and expensive battle. If you choose that route you'll fight your sister and her husband first, and then the winner of your battle will fight the baby's father."

A lose-lose proposition. "Breaking the contract would destroy my relationship with my family. I won't do that. My family is too important to me."

Her attorney nodded. "Then your first order of business is to talk to Beth and Patrick. Tell them what you've discovered. Make sure they still want to adopt this child. Their decision determines your next action."

The idea of confronting Beth and Patrick and the fear of what they'd say made her queasy. Her dream of having Patrick's baby had become a nightmare. Or had it? She'd given up long ago on ever having children of her own.

"If Beth and Patrick no longer want this baby, can I keep it?"

"Your odds of winning either way are not good. The day you signed the waiver to relinquish to your sister and brother-in-law you knowingly entered into this agreement with no intention of parenting this child. Precedents in Texas and California have granted custody to the father in similar situations."

That was not what she wanted to hear. But even if she could keep her baby, what did she know about good parenting? Her parents certainly hadn't set an example to emulate. They'd been gone more than they'd been at home, and when they'd been at home they both tended to be self-centered. Not a pretty picture despite the united front they presented to the world.

"In the meantime," her attorney continued, "I'll pursue legal action against the clinic. Besides their negligence, they've violated so many rules and regulations by releasing your personal information to Mr. Patrick without following proper legal channels that the courts and several regulatory agencies will be occupied for a long time."

"I...I suppose that has to be done to prevent the clinic doing this to someone else. I'll talk to Beth and Patrick this afternoon." Until then she had no idea where she stood.

And that was one conversation she dreaded more than anything she'd ever had to do in her life except for smiling through congratulating the man she loved on marrying her sister.

"Nicole, I'd like to caution you to be civil to Mr. Patrick. In my thirty years of experience I've learned the more contentious the fight becomes, the uglier and more expensive it gets. People forget about doing what's right and start fighting to win at all costs."

Nicole had a sinking feeling Ryan Patrick didn't like losing, and he could afford to fight a lot longer than she could.

Beth and Patrick's silence spoke volumes as did the look they exchanged.

Nicole's stomach cramped with tension while

she waited for their response to her bad news. She dampened her dry lips. "So the baby is still yours…if you want it."

Beth gave her a patient smile. "Of course we want the baby, Nicole. The child is yours and therefore related to us."

Relief loosened the knots in Nicole's muscles.

"Beth, a legal battle could be expensive," Patrick pointed out with his usual pragmatism.

"This baby is a Hightower, dear," Beth countered. "We can't let that man break up our family."

Beth and Patrick shared another long, speaking glance, and a teensy twinge of jealousy pricked Nicole. In the three months she and Patrick had dated before she'd brought him home to meet her parents and siblings she and he had never shared that type of silent communication.

But Beth and Patrick had been married for a long time, Nicole reminded herself. They'd had time to develop those skills. If things had gone differently, if Nicole and Patrick had married as she'd once believed they would, then they would have been the ones with that special bond. Wouldn't they?

But Patrick had preferred her sister, and Nicole wanted him to be happy—even if it wasn't with her. He was one of a kind and the only man who'd ever win her heart. She wasn't like her mother who flitted from one affair to the next searching for some fantasy that didn't exist.

"Beth," Patrick protested.

"Nicole is doing this oh-so-generous thing for me—for *us*—to repay me for looking after her when we were growing up. How could I refuse such a selfless gift? And we do want a baby more than anything, don't we?"

"Right. More than anything."

Did Patrick's tone sound a little bitter and resentful? No. He was just shaken and disappointed by Nicole's news. He'd wanted to be a father and now he wasn't...biologically, anyway. And if he was on edge it was only because he and Beth had been trying to conceive for more than three years. The doctors couldn't find anything wrong with either of them and didn't have a clue to the cause of Beth's unexplained infertility.

Thank God Nicole had conceived on the first try. Otherwise—

You'd have come to your senses.

Lea's nagging voice echoed in Nicole's head. She squelched it. Her assistant didn't understand how much Beth had sacrificed for Nicole to have a regular childhood. Beth had forfeited dates, the prom, going to college among other things to play substitute mom while their globe-trotting parents gallivanted frequently and parented sporadically.

Carrying a child for Beth was the least Nicole could do.

"This could get expensive," Patrick persisted. "You know how much we're already spending on—"

"On getting ready for the baby," Beth replied with a tight smile. "Yes, darling, I know. But Nicole doesn't need to worry about that. She needs someone to take care of her little problem, and taking care of problems is what I do best." Beth turned to Nicole. "Don't worry yourself. Big sister will handle everything. Just like I've always done."

Nicole stifled a wince. Yes, there had been dozens of incidents when Beth had covered for Nicole—none of which Nicole was proud of these days. But somehow Nicole didn't feel as confident in her sister's abilities this time. She wasn't sure that even the mighty Beth could deter Ryan Patrick from his goal.

Her baby would be happy here, Nicole assured herself as she lugged a mountain of insulated food containers past a black Corvette convertible and up Beth's concrete sidewalk between rows of blooming dianthus, begonias and hostas.

Beth and Patrick had bought the large two-story traditional brick home with the lush emerald lawn and white picket fenced backyard with a large family in mind. On any given weekend morning children laughed and played in the neighborhood, riding their bicycles in the cul-de-sac. What more could any child want?

And what more could any woman want for her child?

You've made the right decision. All you have to do is keep Ryan Patrick from upsetting your plan.

The smell of roasting meat filled the air, made her mouth water and thankfully, distracted her from her negative thoughts. She'd been running since her feet hit the floor at five this morning, and she'd barely had time to eat a granola bar for breakfast and swallow her prenatal vitamins.

Letting herself in Beth's side door the way she always did, Nicole checked the kitchen. Empty. That was odd since there was so much to do before the guests arrived at noon. Beth and Patrick were probably getting dressed.

Nicole deposited the food she'd prepared for the party on the counter then put the cold items in the fridge and the warm items in the oven on low heat.

Next on the agenda, the backyard. She stepped onto the stoop, scanned the fenced area and smiled. The weather on this first weekend in September couldn't be more perfect for a picnic. The sun was out, but the expected afternoon high temperature wouldn't be too hot or too cool. This close to autumn it was difficult to anticipate what Knoxville's weather would be when planning weeks or months in advance as she always did.

The additional tables she'd rented had been delivered and set up on the grass. The party supply company had draped the tables with red-and-white checkered cloths and decorated each with a potted blooming red or white geranium as Nicole had instructed. Everything looked bright and cheerful, the perfect place to announce the family would be growing.

A lanky apron- and ball cap–wearing man stood by the massive grill on the edge of the large flagstone patio.

"Good morning," she called out as she approached him. "I'm Nicole Hightower."

He nodded and shook her hand. "Bill Smith. Your rent-a-chef. Great day for a pig pickin'."

"Yes. Do you have everything you need, Bill?"

"Yes, ma'am. Pig's 'bout done. I just put on the chicken. Veggie skewers will go on in a few minutes."

Her stomach rumbled in anticipation, but she had too much to do to get ready for the others' arrivals to take time for a snack. "Excellent. Please help yourself to a soda or iced tea, and don't hesitate to ask me for anything you need."

"Thank you."

She lifted a lid on a nearby cooler and found it filled with ice and canned sodas and bottled water as requested. The second cooler revealed more ice and beer—the varieties her brothers preferred and a couple of magnums of champagne. Perfect. She'd definitely use this party company again. Letting someone else do the grunt work was far better than making Patrick and Beth get up at the crack of dawn to attend to the tasks or racing over here to do it herself.

Beth hated planning events. That's why Nicole always landed the job, and she didn't mind because making sure things ran smoothly was sort of an obsession with her. Now more than ever. She brushed a hand over her belly.

The family picnic was a Labor Day weekend tradition—one she'd started herself after Beth and Patrick had married. If anything needed to run smoothly, today's event did. For the most part her family members got along well, but this year they'd have not only the stress of Nicole's pregnancy news to contend with, but also the pressure of the newest Hightower—a younger half sister none of them had known about until a month ago when she'd shown up on their doorstep and their mother had insisted she be given a job at Hightower Aviation.

Having a living, breathing reminder that her mother was a bit…um, free with her affection had been unsettling to say the least. In the past everyone including their father had pretended not to notice Jacqueline Hightower's indiscretions, and no one talked about her affairs. It would be hard to ignore the situation with her mother's love child at the family gathering. And how had her mother hidden a daughter for twenty-five years, anyway?

Nicole headed back to the house. From the kitchen she followed the sound of Beth's voice toward the living room. Her sister's tone wasn't the one she used when talking to Patrick. Some of the nonfamily party guests must have arrived early. Probably the owner of the convertible.

"The child is not yours." The deep voice stopped Nicole in her tracks in the foyer.

Ryan Patrick was *here.* Talking to Beth.

"The baby is Nicole's," Beth replied.

"Sweetheart," Patrick interjected in that gentle, patient tone of his that Nicole adored. "You do understand that Mr. Patrick is offering us a lot of money to accommodate him."

Nicole's mouth dried and panic caused her

heart to gallop. That devious bastard was trying to bribe her sister and brother-in-law into giving up her baby.

If he brainwashed Beth and Patrick, he could cut Nicole out of the child's life altogether. She wasn't going to let that happen.

She rushed into the room. "How dare you go behind my back?"

Ryan slowly unfolded from the leather wingback chair. His cobalt eyes locked with hers. "I'm going to the ones who have the power to make a decision—the right decision to allow this child to live with his natural father."

She couldn't help noticing the way his charcoal suit, pale blue shirt and crimson tie accentuated his good looks and athletic frame. But pretty is as pretty does, or so one of their many nannies had always said. And what Ryan Patrick was doing was downright ugly.

"I told you, you're not getting this baby."

He shoved the lapels of his suit coat aside and planted his hands on his lean hips. "If you've consulted your attorney, then you know that you don't have any say in the matter."

Unless she went to war with her family. And even then her chances were slim. She glanced at Beth and Patrick and hugged her churning middle. She couldn't start a family feud. Her mother had wreaked enough havoc on them all over the years.

Patience, politeness and perseverance. Her motto echoed in her head. Every problem had a solution. All she had to do was find it. In the meantime, she'd have to be nice to the jerk if she wanted any chance of wringing a positive outcome from this situation. She hated sucking up to blowhards, but she'd mastered the skill.

"Could I speak with you outside a moment?" she said through a smile stretched so tightly her cheeks hurt.

Ryan gestured toward the door.

Trying to ignore the delicious tang of his cologne, she accompanied him to the center hall then led the way to the back door. He reached past her to open it for her. She marched across the backyard, heading toward the gazebo in the back corner of the lot with Ryan close on her heels. Too close.

Inside the jasmine-draped structure she put as much distance between them as the shelter would permit before facing him. How could she make him see reason?

"Do you have any brothers and sisters, Ryan?" His name felt awkward on her tongue. But she couldn't keep calling him Mr. Patrick. Each time she said his last name she thought of the man inside the house—the man whose baby she should be carrying.

"No."

So much for appealing to his family nature. He didn't have one. "Then you can't possibly understand how important it is for me to have this child for my sister."

"That's irrelevant. It's not her kid. It's mine."

She couldn't argue with facts. She took a calming breath and tried a different tactic. "She has been yearning for a baby for years, and she'll love this one as if it were hers. How much experience do you have with children?"

"I'll learn what I need to know."

The stubborn blockhead. She had to find a way to convince him that the baby would be better off with Beth and Patrick. But how? The answer was almost too easy. She smiled.

"As you can see from the setup, we're having a party in a few minutes. It will be mostly family with a few friends and neighbors thrown into the mix. Please join us."

His eyes narrowed. "Why?"

"So you can see what a great life Beth and Patrick can give this baby. The child will be surrounded by a loving family. He or she will have aunts and uncles and soon, cousins. My sister-in-law is expecting to deliver just a few months before me."

"You won't change my mind."

Maybe not. But it was a risk she had to take if she wanted to be a part of her baby's life. "All I ask is that you keep an open mind and see what you're determined to deny this child. Join us, Ryan…unless you're allergic to good food and good company."

He stiffened at her implied challenge and accepted her dare with a slight dip of his chin. But his drilling stare warned her he wasn't going to make this easy for her. For the next four hours she would have her work cut out for her in convincing him to change his mind.

Her baby's future and her role in it depended on her success in making Ryan Patrick agree to go away empty-handed.

Forty people milled about Beth and Patrick Ryan's backyard. But only one held Ryan's attention. Nicole Hightower.

He shouldn't find her attractive. She wasn't his type. He liked his women curvy and soothing. Nicole bordered on too slender and restless. Not only could she not stand still for more than thirty seconds, but also her lean build didn't include the matronly "breeding hips" he'd chosen for his surrogate. Yet he had no problem imagining her nursing a baby at the small, but firm-looking breasts outlined by her sundress.

Not a thought he needed to entertain since that would not happen with his child. His child would be bottle-fed by a nanny from day one.

Nicole's aqua eyes turned his way, hitting him with another megavolt jolt of awareness. She'd nailed him with a similar glance several times this afternoon, and he couldn't prevent the unwelcome gut-jarring reaction each time their gazes met.

He didn't want a relationship with her other than a contractual one. If all went according to his plan, she'd have his kid, hand it over and get out of his life. He didn't want her underfoot and interfering. He didn't need the drama.

Nicole indicated his beer with a slight nod. He shook his head. Drinking to excess didn't mix well with sexual attraction unless he intended to end up in bed with the object of his attention. He'd done that often enough in the past couple of decades to push his father into concocting the stupid stipulation that Ryan prove his stability and maturity if he wanted to take over the reins of Patrick Architectural upon his father's retirement next summer. If Ryan failed, his father had threatened to sell the firm. That made ignoring the chemistry between him and Nicole imperative because another short-term affair—no matter how hot it might burn before it fizzled out—wouldn't help his cause.

A breeze lifted Nicole's long hair away from her face. He preferred the wavy caramel-colored strands loose and swishing between her shoulder blades instead of twisted up on her head the way they had been the day he'd confronted her at her office.

Not that his preferences counted.

Genetically, she should produce a good-looking kid. She was more attractive than the surrogate he'd hired. Her face was fine-boned and full-lipped, her smile quick and frequent—except when she looked at him. Then the stretch of her lips was slow and forced as if having him here were a pain in the rear.

Another thing he'd noticed this afternoon, Nicole was a toucher. Every time someone got close enough, she reached out and brushed a hand over their arm or shoulder or kissed a cheek. That's why he'd kept his distance. He didn't want a repeat of the zap she'd delivered with that first handshake the day they'd met. Chemistry was great. Unless it was unwanted. Then it was nothing but trouble.

He scanned the yard, passing over each of the Hightowers. He'd bet Nicole would look exactly like her mother in forty years. She possessed the same slender build, same features. Behavior-wise, other than the high energy level, Mamma Hightower was the opposite of her daughter. Whereas Nicole was friendly, but reserved, her mother was flirtatious, gregarious and sexually aware of every move she made in that way well-maintained wealthy older women exhibited when they'd been the type to bring men to their knees in their younger days.

Nicole's father, a silent loner who nursed his imported beer in the shade of a tall oak tree, only spoke to those who sought him out. Her older twin brothers looked identical, but one was a player and the other appeared to be an unhappily married man with an eye that often strayed from his pregnant wife to the female guests.

Ryan's gaze skimmed over neighbors and other company until it landed on Beth and Patrick Ryan huddled in the corner of the patio. They were arguing. Again. Ryan had caught several heated exchanges between them during the past three hours.

Nicole might believe this was the perfect setup for raising a child, but Ryan sensed trouble in this suburban, cookie-cutter paradise. The tension between the couple was palpable from fifty feet away, and it had been even more obvious when he'd presented his offer before the party. Just one more reason to make damned sure he got full custody. He didn't want his kid to be a bone of contention in an ugly divorce the way he'd been. And he'd bet his Corvette, his boat and his motorcycle the Ryans would land in divorce court sooner than later.

Beth reminded him of his mother. She wore the same self-suffering martyr attitude his mother had pulled in the years after she'd packed up a ten-year-old Ryan and moved away from her husband. Millicent Patrick had spent the next eight years using Ryan as a weapon against his father and bitching about his father's mistress—work.

Her complaints had fallen on deaf ears. A love of architecture was something he and his father had had in common even back when Ryan had been a snot-nosed kid. For as far back as he could remember, Ryan had spent hours beside his father's drafting table asking questions, begging to be allowed to "help." His father had always indulged him until the separation after which he'd had little time for his only son.

Work was the only mistress he and his father respected or committed to for the long haul. Women couldn't be trusted or counted on. A lesson he'd learned the hard way compliments of his ex-wife, the lying, cheating bitch.

His gaze shifted to the youngest Hightower. She interested him because as much as she resembled her mother and Nicole, she didn't fit in. The roar of her Harley splitting the silence of the neighborhood had been his first clue. Like him, she was an outsider here. Not even Nicole's frequent attempts at drawing her sister into the crowd could breach the gap between her and the rest of the siblings. And Nicole seemed to be the only one making an effort to include her sister.

The Hightower in question looked up, caught his eye and headed in his direction. Her black leather boots and jeans-covered legs crossed the lawn with a long stride. In the past the rebel in her would have called to the rebel in him. But for some reason, her wild side didn't twitch his interest today.

She stopped in front of him. "You don't look like one of Beth's snooty neighbors."

Ryan smiled. He'd made the same assumption about the guests' attitudes. He offered his hand. "Ryan Patrick and, no, I don't live in the area."

Her eyebrows rose when she heard his name, but she didn't comment. Her handshake was firm and brief with no sparks despite her resemblance to her sister. "Lauren Lynch."

She looked enough like Nicole that he would have sworn they were closely related. "You're not a Hightower?"

"Jacqueline is my mother, but William isn't my father. My father died a couple of months ago. And before you strain your brain trying to unravel that long, boring story, my mother had an affair with a Hightower Aviation pilot. I'm the byproduct. She delivered me, left me with my dad and returned to her husband and other children like a good little wife."

That explained the tension between Lauren and the Hightower siblings. "I'm sorry for your loss."

She shrugged. "Thanks. Losing my dad was

hard, but his passing gave me the opportunity to meet a family I didn't know I had. So what brings you here? Are you a Hightower Aviation client?"

He wasn't ready to reveal the truth. "Not yet, but I'm considering contracting the company."

Access to a plane would make his life easier since he traveled the country on a regular basis. He definitely wanted to contract one of the Hightowers. But not for flying.

"Married?" Lauren asked.

He gave her credit for being direct. "Not anymore. You?"

"No way. Never have been. Probably never will be. Do you have any children?"

"Not yet."

Lauren glanced down at her beer bottle then back up at him through lashes as long and thick as her sister's. "Can I give you a hint?"

About what? "Sure."

"Nicole's probably the most decent one in the bunch. Maybe even the only decent Hightower. But she's going to be a hard nut to crack because... Well, she just is. I'll let you figure out the whys. Stick with her. She's worth it."

Were all women born with a matchmaking gene?

"What makes you think I'm interested in Nicole?"

Lauren grinned and sipped her beer. "Could be the way you've been watching her all afternoon."

Guilty. But how else was he going to learn about the mother of his child? He searched for her. Nicole had joined her sister and brother-in-law and was currently engaged in a hushed but animated conversation. Nicole covered her belly with one hand. Her gaze bounced over the crowd and landed on Ryan. He didn't know what her sister had said to upset her, but the distress on her face was clear. Adrenaline shot through his system.

"Go ahead," Lauren prompted.

"Go ahead and what?"

"Ride to her rescue. You know you want to."

Smart girl. "Is Nicole the type to need rescuing?"

Lauren grimaced. "Let's just say if I were her, I would have told this bunch of leeches to go to hell a long time ago. But she's the one deputized to maintain the peace."

Lauren was full of interesting factoids. One of these days he'd buy her dinner and pick her brain. "Nice meeting you, Lauren."

"You, too, Ryan. And good luck."

He wasn't going to need luck. He had the law on his side.

His feet carried him across the grass to the trio. "Problem?"

Beth shook her head and gave him a disingenuous smile—the only kind he'd seen from her to date. "We've decided against announcing Nicole's pregnancy today."

He liked the sound of that. The longer they delayed, the more time he'd have to prepare for the possibility of the entire Hightower clan siding against him. The extra time would give him time to plot a new strategy.

But why would the decision to keep the news under wraps upset Nicole? He searched her face, but didn't find his answer.

Little did she know, she'd done him a favor by showing him the dissension amongst the Hightowers, and she'd given him ammunition toward suing for sole custody.

He needed to divide and conquer the trio wanting a piece of his kid, starting with the weakest link.

Nicole's brother-in-law, the greedy bastard.

Three

"Ryan Patrick is here for your lunch appointment."

Lea's announcement made Nicole's already stretched nerves snarl. Her fingers spasmed on the keyboard, filling the document on her monitor with a spew of gibberish.

She punched the intercom button. "We don't have a lunch appointment."

"Yes, you do. He called and I scheduled it."

She wanted to strangle her assistant. "What does he want?"

"There's only one way to find out." The

smirk in Lea's voice came through the speaker loud and clear.

Nicole saved her work, closed the file and rose. She'd fix the gibberish later. She wasn't capable now. "Send him in. But Lea, don't make any more surprise appointments for me. And stop matchmaking. Your record proves you suck at it."

Over the past few years Lea had made a determined effort to find the man who could make Nicole forget Patrick. Her friend couldn't accept that such a man didn't exist.

Unlike Nicole's fickle mother who changed her lovers as often as she touched up her manicure, Nicole would only love once in her lifetime. She'd rather be alone than with the wrong man—or a series of them. And she was very careful not to let herself board that crazy lust-love-crash roller coaster. Whenever she realized she was in line for that ride she stepped aside. No more heartache for her.

Moments later her door swung inward and Ryan filled the opening. He wore a black suit with a white shirt and a cobalt tie that matched his eyes. Her stomach fluttered.

Who would her child take after? Him or her?

The man would make beautiful babies.

Never mind. Looks don't matter. A healthy baby is all you're after.

"Nicole." He nodded his dark head in a greeting and his eyes raked over her, making her very conscious of how her raspberry-pink V-neck, wraparound dress clung to her pregnancy swollen breasts. "Ready?"

His low-pitched voice scraped over her nerve endings like an emery board, leaving her feeling raw and exposed and strangely out of sorts.

"Why are you here, Ryan?"

He pushed the door closed between him and Lea. "Because I'd like to know something about the woman carrying my child besides the sparse raw data in the clinic's file. I imagine you have questions concerning my health and history, too."

Now that he mentioned it, she did. With Patrick she hadn't needed to ask because she'd already known everything about him.

Do this for Beth and for the baby you're carrying for her.

What was it the old cliché said? Keep your

friends close and your enemies closer. Ryan Patrick qualified as the latter. He definitely threatened all she held dear. And the only way she could learn more about him was by spending time with him.

"I can give you a couple of hours."

"That's all we'll need."

She grabbed her purse and crossed the room. He opened the door as she approached and pressed his hand to her waist to guide her through as she passed by him. Every cell in her body snapped to attention startling her so much she bumped the door frame.

He caught her upper arm and steadied her, his fingers branding a circle around her biceps. "Careful."

Their gazes met. Her heart stuttered. Why did *he* have to have this effect on her? The man was an arrogant ass.

You're carrying his baby. Of course you're going to have a reaction to him.

Nicole shook off his hold.

Lea grinned unrepentantly. "Have a great lunch. Don't rush back. I have everything under control."

Nicole frowned at her assistant. "I'll be back in time for my next appointment."

"Your two o'clock postponed until four. I can reschedule him until tomorrow, if you'd like."

Nicole glared a warning. "Don't you dare."

"Well, take it easy. You have plenty of time."

Not what she needed Ryan to hear when she wanted an excuse to cut lunch short. But she bit back her reservations and accompanied him outside to his Corvette. He opened the door for her. She avoided his touch and slid into the leather seat.

He climbed into the driver's side, making the luxurious sports car feel crowded. His scent filled her nostrils and his nearness addled her nerves.

"Why did your sister failing to announce your pregnancy upset you?" he asked as he started the car.

Give the man points for being perceptive. But her feelings were none of his business. "It didn't."

He cut her a hard look before pulling onto the road. "I don't like or respect liars."

She gasped, gritted her teeth and focused on her three *P*'s. *Patience, politeness, perseverance.*

"I like things to go according to schedule. Beth changed the schedule at the last minute. That's all. No big deal."

But it was. A week ago Beth had been ecstatic about the upcoming announcement and ready to blurt out the news at any second. Waiting until the party had driven her up the wall, but she'd claimed she wanted the announcement to be memorable. So why had her sister suddenly developed cold feet? Was she having doubts about adopting this baby now that she knew it wasn't her husband's? Or maybe Patrick was the one with doubts.

Nicole caught herself examining Ryan's cleanly chiseled profile and the soft line of his lips. She felt the stirrings of something deep inside her abdomen and clamped down on the unwelcome feelings. She was not attracted to him. She was merely curious to know if her—*Beth's* baby would inherit those great genes.

She turned away from his face to look out the window. He drove through downtown, past the university and toward Volunteer Landing, a riverfront section of the Tennessee River flanked by a park, restaurants, pricey condos and the sprawling hospital complex. On summer weekends tourists and locals filled the concrete stands along the water to watch the water ski and wakeboard competitions. It had been ages since she'd taken the time to attend one of the events.

But instead of parking at the Landing, he crossed the Henley Street Bridge and turned into an exclusive gated condominium complex. A guard waved him through the entrance. The tall, modern waterfront structure had expansive windows and long cantilevered porches. This wasn't a commercial property.

A parade of prickles marched up her spine. "Where are we going?"

"My place."

Too private. Too personal. Too…everything. "I don't think that's a good idea."

He parked in the ground level area beneath the condos beside a wicked-looking black motorcycle and turned off the engine. Both his and the motorcycle's parking spaces were labeled 10A.

"Would you prefer to discuss our unusual

situation across the river at Calhoun's or Ruth's Chris where we might be overheard?"

As much as she liked both restaurants, he'd made a good point. "Um…no. The motorcycle is yours?"

"Yes."

That made him a risk-taker. Not good parent material.

A vision of him straddling the machine and dressed in black leather flashed in her head. The confines of the car suddenly felt stuffy. She shoved open the door, climbed out and let the breeze blowing off the water cool her hot skin.

He led her toward a bank of elevators. Her heels rapped out a beat on the concrete almost as rapidly as her heart knocked in her chest. Inside the elevator he punched the button for the top floor, and the brushed steel cubicle shot upward quickly and noiselessly.

The doors opened onto a spacious atrium-style foyer with a modern peaked glass ceiling similar to the pyramid shapes at the Louvre. Natural light flooded the plant-filled space, and a fountain gurgled in the center. Four doors opened off opposite sides of the octagonal area.

"This is nice." Too modern for her traditional tastes, but still attractive with its curved teak benches and pebbled pathways.

"Thanks. I designed the building."

Extremely pricey waterfront real estate. Penthouse level. Her worry multiplied as she filed the information away. Neither she nor Beth and Patrick could afford the kind of lengthy legal brawl Ryan apparently could. Not that any of them were hurting for cash, but they weren't in league with someone who could afford multimillion-dollar accommodations.

Ryan unlocked a door on the river side of the building and gestured for her to precede him. Dreading the hour to come, she gathered her courage and entered Ryan Patrick's domain.

His entry opened directly into a huge living area with a wall of floor-to-ceiling windows. Dark slate floors gleamed beneath her feet. The stone might be beautiful, but it would be hard and cold and hazardous for a child learning to crawl or walk. The urban industrial upscale furnishings would also be problematic with their sharp brushed steel edges and glass table tops.

She crossed to the window and looked down. A wave of vertigo hit her, and she staggered back to assess Ryan's space from a safer distance away from the glass. Outside to her left a stark, Plexiglas-railed patio jutted from the dining area beside her to the far end of the building. The modern stone sculptures, plant holders and glass-and-steel dining set couldn't keep the slab from looking like a giant diving platform from which you could tumble right over the edge.

The condo suited him perfectly. Dark. Edgy. Cold. Dangerous.

Taking tiny, careful steps she forced herself to return to the window and a clear view of World's Fair Park with its Sunsphere. The Tennessee River drifted lazily past ten stories below. Volunteer Landing stretched along the opposite bank with its broad walkway and manmade water features. The tourist paddle boat, a favorite for weddings, clung to the shore upstream.

In front of Ryan's complex on this side of the river a long boat dock floated parallel to the tiny green space. Watercraft of assorted sizes filled the slips.

"Is one of those yours, too?" She pointed to the boats.

"Third from the right."

She knew enough about water sports from her brothers' exploits to recognize the long, low boat had been built for speed.

Ryan's place was a mother's nightmare. Add in his expensive and risky toys and the possibility of her child growing up here scared her witless. "Your home isn't suitable for children."

"Why?"

She startled at his nearness and spun to find him standing only inches away—far too close. She hadn't heard him cross the room. She side-stepped to put a few feet between them.

"Besides the fact that you apparently have a death wish with your need-for-speed toys?"

His muscles tensed. "I'm careful."

She rolled her eyes at the ridiculous statement. "There's no fencing to keep a child from falling off the dock and into the murky water, and there isn't nearly enough grass for a child to run and play. Children need playgrounds and yards."

"City kids around the world manage without acre lots."

"Are there any other children in this building?"

His jaw shifted. He shrugged. "I don't know."

"A child needs playmates. Beth and Patrick's place is better suited."

His intense blue gaze held hers. "Forget your sister and her husband for a moment. This lunch is about you and me."

Her pulse stuttered. "How so?"

He advanced a step. She retreated one. "I've been tested for HIV and every other sexually transmitted disease and I'm clean. Have you been tested?"

Startled by his blunt question, she flinched. "No. There was no need."

"You're a virgin?"

Her cheeks burned. "Of course not. I'm twenty-eight."

But she was careful. More careful than anyone knew. Because she didn't want to end up like her mother.

"I required testing from my other surrogate candidates. I'll set up an appointment for you."

Appalled, she sputtered. "You'll do no such thing. I'm not one of your candidates."

"No. You're the woman carrying my child. That makes a clean bill of health even more critical. Get tested voluntarily or I'll get a court order."

She snapped her gaping mouth closed. "You can't do that."

"I've already spoken to my attorney. I can. This is my kid. I have a vested interest in his welfare."

Nicole wanted to slap her hands over her ears, but she refrained. "Stop saying that. Your contribution was an accident. You weren't there. You had nothing to do with it. And if the clinic hadn't broken the law and given you my confidential information then you wouldn't even know my name."

"Irrelevant. I know who you are, and I'm not going away. Do us both a favor and don't make our lawyers rich." He turned, releasing her from the tension of his total concentration, removed his suit coat and tossed it over the back of a minimalist leather chair.

She took the opportunity to move away from him. He made her uncomfortable. Why? She had no idea. She dealt with powerful men on a daily basis—men who were in-her-face obnoxious and demanding. She easily kept her cool with them. It wasn't as easy with Ryan.

Because he's threatening your—Beth's—*baby. That makes it personal.*

He faced her again, unbuttoned his cuffs then started rolling up his sleeves. "Do you smoke?"

The slow revelation of a tanned, muscled forearm riveted her attention. "No."

"Drink alcohol?"

"Occasionally. But not at all now that I'm expecting."

"Have you had more than five sexual partners?"

Offended, she stiffened. "That is none of your business. Take me back to my office. Now."

He finished rolling up his second sleeve and parked his hands on those lean hips. "These are standard questions from the fertility clinic questionnaire which they neglected to have you complete. You have the right to ask the same questions of me. And you should."

As rude and insulting as he'd been, he was also correct and fair-minded. She hated that a virtual stranger had the right to pry into her personal business. But what if he ended up sharing custody of this child with Beth and Patrick? She—*correction*—Beth and Patrick needed to know everything about him.

"The clinic doesn't accept donations from or inseminate HIV-positive clients. If you'd done your research, you would know that."

"They also claim they don't make mistakes."

Point to Ryan. She sighed. "I've had less than five partners. You?"

"More than five. But I've been careful. Are you seeing anyone now?"

"No." This was worse than a blind date. "Are you? Is there a woman who'll have problems with my pregnancy?"

"No."

"A man?"

His venomous look should have dropped her on the spot, but she had to ask since his solo quest for a child was an unusual one.

His blue eyes scanned her body, leaving a ripple of sensation in their wake. "Do you have any habits that might aversely affect my child's well-being?"

"I never would have agreed to carry this child for Beth if I did, and I don't take any drugs except for the prenatal vitamins."

"Good. Let's eat." He walked away.

"I'd rather go back to work." Or even as far away as Alaska to get away from him.

"You need to eat for yourself and the baby," he called over his shoulder.

Unfortunately, he was right again. Rather than wait for him in his austere living room, she followed him into a spacious kitchen with stone countertops, glass-front upper cabinets and top-of-the-line stainless steel appliances. As much as he'd already unsettled her stomach with his intrusive questions, she doubted she'd be able to swallow a bite.

He pulled a casserole dish from the top of the double oven. A delicious tomato-and-garlic scent filled the air. Her stomach growled in anticipation. "You assumed a lot by preparing a meal before I agreed to go out with you."

"We both have the kid's best interest at heart, and from what I've read about you, you're intelligent enough to know we need to have this discussion. Take a seat and help yourself. It's vegetable lasagna."

He had no idea how close she'd come to refusing his "invitation." She crossed to the glass-topped iron table. He set the rectangular dish on a trivet in the center then returned to pull a loaf of bread from the bottom oven. He sliced the bread, tossed the slices into a basket and brought the basket to the table.

She could get used to a man who was good in the kitchen.

Oh no you won't.

Next he retrieved a bowl of marinated green beans with grape tomatoes and a pitcher of iced tea from the refrigerator and placed them in the middle of the table, then he sat across from her and filled their glasses.

Nicole's stomach did one of those weird things it had been doing a lot lately. In a split second it went from not remotely interested in food to ravenous. She loaded her plate and as soon as Ryan had done the same, she dug into the lasagna. The tangy, sauce made her eyes roll back in pleasure, and the thick chunks of eggplant and mushroom tasted better than anything she'd eaten in ages.

She ate for several minutes before looking up and finding his gaze on her. Embarrassed by her unladylike appetite, she paused with her fork halfway to her mouth—the mouth his eyes had focused on. "You know how to cook?"

"My grandmother made sure I learned."

She'd always envied her friends whose men enjoyed sharing the kitchen with them. But that kind of domestic bliss wasn't on her agenda. "This is very good."

"Thank you." He watched her tuck a tomato between her lips and something changed in his eyes. Something that caused her stomach muscles to tense and her pulse to flutter.

She fought off the sensation and concentrated on the things she didn't like about him. His bossiness. His risky hobbies. His determination to deprive her of her child.

"Despite your domestic skills, between your motorcycle and your boat and from what I've read about you, you're nowhere near responsible enough to raise a child."

"You shouldn't believe what you read in the gossip columns."

How could she ignore what her Google search had revealed? Look at him. What woman wouldn't want him? Except her, that is. He was smart, successful and wealthy. Hadn't her brothers proven that men constantly bombarded with women tended to be selfish and far from good father material?

"Do you or do you not trade in your women more often than most people charge their cell-phone batteries? A child needs security and stability."

"I haven't been involved in a long-term relationship lately, if that's what you're asking. Have you?"

"My love life is none of your business."

"It is if your habits could endanger my kid's health."

Her mouth opened and closed like a goldfish, but she couldn't manage to dredge up a blistering comeback. Once again, as ugly as his comment might have been, his concern was valid. "That isn't an issue."

"I want a copy of your medical records and to attend every doctor's appointment with you."

She bit her tongue. Pain stabbed her mouth. "What?"

"You'll need to transfer your records to the obstetrical practice I've chosen."

"Are you out of your mind? You can't make those decisions for me."

"I want to track his development. And this obstetrical group is the best in the region."

She shoved her plate aside. "First of all, *he* might be a *she.* Second, I have my own doctor. I've been seeing her for years, and I'm not changing. You can't make me."

He weighed her words as if debating arguing. "Is he or she board certified?"

"Of course. I wouldn't go to a hack—especially now. I'll have my doctor fax you a report after each visit."

"Not good enough. I want to be able to address questions as they arise and see the ultrasound scans."

Any child would be lucky to have a parent so interested. If only hers had been, but her father had been too busy with his gambling buddies.

"I'll check with my doctor, but I think she'll

agree to meet with you. I also want to make sure Beth and Patrick are comfortable with your intrusion."

Not that either of them had attended her appointments thus far. Their absence had surprised Nicole. But maybe the obstetrical appointments were painful reminders of Beth's inability to conceive.

"They'll have to deal with it. Get used to it, Nicole. I will be a part of this child's life with or without your voluntary consent. And I won't be parked in the waiting room at the doctor's office. I'll be right by your side during every examination."

Four

Ryan's audacity astounded Nicole. He was backing her into a corner, and she really didn't like it.

She could feel her muscles tensing, her heart pounding and her hands trembling. She silently chanted her three *P's*. Her mantra didn't have its usual calming effect. The urge to tell him to go to hell nearly overcame her good manners, but volatile reactions never solved a problem. They only exacerbated the situation, and alienating him was the last thing she needed to do.

"You can't impose on my private doctor's appointments."

"Would you like to bet on that? Your exams are also my child's exams. I have the right to make sure you're following doctor's orders and not endangering my kid."

She crumpled the cloth napkin in her lap and her toes curled in her shoes. "I would never do that!"

It took everything Nicole had to rein in her temper. For Patrick and Beth's sake, for her baby's sake, she had to find a solution—a peaceable solution. She excelled at finding ways to make the impossible happen at work. Wasn't she known as the go-to girl? But compromise ideas were scarce now.

She'd learned that whenever a problem was this complex it helped to break it down into manageable increments and address each component separately. She needed time and distance away from Ryan to get her thoughts in line.

Carefully pushing her chair back from the table, she took a deep breath and then rose to her feet. "Thank you for lunch, but I'd like to leave now."

He stood more slowly. “You haven’t finished your lunch.”

“I don’t think I can eat another bite. Morning sickness.” More like man sickness.

“It’s not morning.”

“The baby doesn’t wear a Rolex.” Ryan did—an expensive gold model like her father had gambled away at a casino. She remembered the screaming match that had ensued when her mother found out.

“I’ll drive you.”

She dropped her napkin beside her plate. “I’d rather call a taxi.”

“We haven’t finished our discussion.”

She couldn’t possibly remain polite in his company. “There’s no need. Please have your physician fax your health records to my office.”

“Mine?” His dark eyebrows winged upward.

“Yes. Yours. As you pointed out, I—we have every right to know if this baby will inherit something from you that might affect the pregnancy or delivery.”

“I told you I was healthy.”

“And you expect me to take the word of a

stranger?" She threw his words back at him, and then smothered a wince.

That wasn't nice, Nicole.

But maybe if he realized how ridiculously intrusive he was being then he'd back off.

"I'll take care of it. But I'm not calling a cab for you. I brought you. I'll take you back." His inflexible tone and rock-hard jaw warned her arguing would be a waste of time.

Some battles weren't worth fighting. As long as she won the war—and she would win—she could concede this one. "Fine. Lead the way."

"Before you go, I have one more request."

Her insides snarled into a tense knot at the calculating glint in his baby blues. Her control was already teetering on the edge. One teensy shove and she'd lose her temper.

"If you find my home unsuitable, then help me find another one."

She blinked and swallowed, not liking the direction of his thinking. "Why would I do that? And why would you want me to?"

"Because we both want my child to be raised in a safe environment."

My child. The words raised her hackles, her temperature and her heart rate each time he said them. But at the same time, she couldn't help but be impressed that he cared enough to make the effort to provide a better environment. "A real-estate agent would be more knowledgeable."

"Without a doubt. I'll engage one to find the houses, but she won't have a personal stake in my decision. You might as well know I intend to sue for sole custody, but worse case scenario, I'll end up sharing with Beth and Patrick. Either way, I'm looking for a safe place, and I know you have a vested interest in my selection."

He'd certainly laid his cards on the table. And while part of her respected him for his honesty, the other hated knowing his strategy.

Her lawyer had confirmed the courts would be unlikely to deny him some form of connection. If the worst case scenario he mentioned came about, the child's welfare came first. And she'd rather her child live anywhere than here in a place where his or her safety would always be at risk.

"I'll help you find a house. But don't believe for one minute that equates to me accepting the inevitability of you as a parent to my—*this* baby. You are not parent material."

One corner of his mouth quirked up with stomach-flipping, breath-catching effect. "Guess I'll have to prove you wrong."

"Is that your latest floozy?" Harlan Patrick spit the question from the opposite side of Ryan's desk.

Ryan glanced at the photo lying on the top of the open file he'd composed on Hightower Aviation. He'd printed the professional shot of Nicole from the Hightower Web page. The photographer hadn't managed to catch the fire in her aquamarine eyes or the golden glints in her light brown hair.

He wasn't ready to share his surrogacy plan with his father yet or discuss how it had gone wrong. "I don't sleep with every woman I meet."

His father snorted in disbelief. He'd always believed the worst of his son—probably because until recently Ryan had given him reason to. Ryan had spent a lot of time acting obnoxious as a kid hoping his mother would get sick of his shenanigans and send him back to his father, but his strategy hadn't worked. By the time he'd gone off to college the rebel pattern had become a habit.

But his partying and rebelling days were over. And while he would never deliberately deceive anyone, he wasn't above letting his father's tendency to jump to conclusions work in his favor for once.

Nicole Hightower was exactly the kind of woman his father wanted him to marry. Ryan had no intentions of marrying anyone, but if his father saw him and Nicole together and believed there might be a long-term relationship in Ryan's future, then he wasn't going to correct him. At least not now. There would be ample time for that later—after his father handed over the presidency of Patrick Architectural.

"Her name is Nicole Hightower. She's a client services manager for Hightower Aviation Management Corporation." He removed Nicole's picture from the file, laid it to the side of his blotter and passed the folder to his father. "We should consider fractional ownership or leasing a plane from HAMC."

"Why? So you can have another damned expensive toy? My God, Ryan, you risk your neck with no thought to who will take over Patrick Architectural if you kill yourself."

The repetitive lecture that had launched Ryan's current campaign set his teeth on edge.

"You already have a thirty-thousand-dollar motorcycle and a sixty-thousand-dollar boat. What next? A five-million-dollar plane? And I suppose you want to get your pilot's license, too."

Ryan bit back his irritation. "I don't want or need a pilot's license. Hightower maintains and staffs the plane. Patrick Architectural flies associates all over the country on a last-minute basis, and we pay a premium for those tickets. Hightower guarantees that if we contract their services we could have our plane and their pilot on the runway within four hours or less."

"Pretentious waste of money."

"They'd fly us directly to our destination without connecting flights, layovers, limited flight schedules and other inconveniences. They can even land the jets at smaller airports when there isn't a large hub near our destination."

"The costs of owning a plane would be prohibitive." His father dismissed the idea without even looking at the data. Typical.

"Not necessarily. I've talked to a Hightower representative. There are a variety of options. We can buy a plane outright, lease or even buy a specified number of flight hours per month or year in a pay-as-you-go program. The best deal is fractional ownership which means we'd only buy a one-eighth to one-sixteenth share, but a plane would always be available to us. When the size of our team required it, we'd be able to request a smaller or larger aircraft.

"The company makes it work for us. Their motto is Comfort, Convenience and Time Savings. From what I've heard, they deliver that promise."

He rolled to his feet, circled the desk and tapped the folder in his father's hands. "Turn to the chart on page six. Take a look at the data I asked Cindy to compile."

God bless his assistant's fascination with tracking the most ludicrous factoids.

He waited until his father did as asked. "This graph catalogs how much time our employees have lost over the past year on layovers, flight delays, inconvenient connector flights and last-minute cancellations or reroutings. They're on the clock during that lost travel time. There's your waste of money. Averaged out, our total travel expense comes close to covering the monthly cost for fractional ownership, but without the added benefit of a tax write-off and convenience. Access to our own plane would allow us to expand globally."

His father's gaze sharpened as the idea took root and the automatic rejection to any idea Ryan presented faded. Harlan ran a finger down the sheet as he perused the data a second time.

Ryan shoved his hands in his pockets and walked to the window overlooking downtown Knoxville. "The packet includes Hightower Aviation's brochure. Read the documentation and you'll see that a plane could be an expedient asset for us. If we set up the aircraft as a mobile office complete with wireless Internet and a fax machine, we could work midair and-or meet with clients on the way to a site. A bedroom suite containing a full bath is also available so we can fly overnight and arrive rested and ready to work first thing in the morning—negating the additional expense of a hotel room. An airplane is not a frivolous waste of money."

"And the girl?"

His father wasn't stupid. Ryan had known he wouldn't be so easily distracted. He faced his father, who also happened to be his mentor and sometimes his enemy. "As our client services representative Nicole would be our main contact. When we need to travel we'd call her directly and tell her our requirements—right down to which meals we'd want served on the flight. It's her job to make it happen."

"You think she'd be assigned to us?"

"I'm told she's the best they have. We would make her part of any deal we strike."

His father tapped the edge of the folder on Ryan's desk. "I'll give it a look, but I doubt it's feasible."

Another wave of irritation washed over Ryan. "If it weren't feasible, I wouldn't have presented the idea to you."

"We'll see."

Ryan smothered his frustration. History had shown his father would do everything he could to prove Ryan's idea a bad one. Only when he couldn't, would he come around.

Ryan looked forward to the day his father retired, leaving Ryan as president of Patrick Architectural. But first he had to prove he could handle the job, or his father would sell the firm his great-grandfather had started right out from under him.

Days like today convinced Nicole she was doing the right thing. She sank onto her sofa and pried her pumps off her swollen feet Saturday afternoon with a smile on her face.

Seeing Beth's excitement as they raced around Knoxville shopping the baby goods sales filled Nicole with a sense of purpose and rightness. This would work out. All she had to do was keep the fly out of the ointment. The fly being Ryan Patrick.

Thinking of him made her smile fade. The three days without seeing or hearing from him had been good and relaxing. She'd even forgotten about him several times. For a few minutes.

Exhaustion slammed her suddenly from out of nowhere. During the past month her morning sickness had been minimal and manageable, but she hadn't been able to eliminate the fatigue. When it hit, it hit hard and fast. Yawning, she stretched out on the cushions and pulled a floral woven throw over her legs.

She was floating in that hazy just-before-sleep stage when her doorbell rang. Forcing open her eyes, she blinked at the cuckoo clock on the wall until her eyes focused on the hands. Beth had dropped her off barely ten minutes ago. Her sister must have forgotten something.

Nicole levered her body upright, trudged barefoot to the front door of her town house and yanked it open. Instead of Beth, Ryan Patrick stood on her welcome mat—a most unwelcome sight. Surprise knocked her back a step, and her warm and fuzzy good mood evaporated instantly.

Her lack of shoes gave him the height advantage. She had to tip her head way back to look at him. He looked gorgeous in a black polo shirt with his bright blue eyes and an afternoon beard shadowing his angular jaw.

"How did you get my home address?"

"Your clinic file." His thorough head-to-toe inspection made her yearn to smooth her hair and check her makeup which was ridiculous considering she didn't care what he thought of her appearance.

How dare he invade her personal space? Antagonism prickled over her. She tried to rein it in. Tried and failed miserably. She could feel her face getting hotter. "Did you need something so urgently you couldn't call?"

"I called and left a message. You didn't reply. I don't have your cell-phone number."

And he never would. "I've been out all morning and just returned home. I haven't checked my machine yet. What do you want?"

Ooh. That hadn't sounded friendly. *Tamp the hostility, Nicole.*

"We have an appointment to look at a couple of houses this afternoon."

"We?"

"You agreed to help me search."

So she had. But today? She needed time to prepare for his company and time to concoct excuses to avoid him. "And if I'm busy this afternoon?"

"Are you?"

She'd love a nap, but admitting weakness to the enemy was never good strategy. Times like this made her miss the caffeine she'd given up for her pregnancy. She needed a jolt to put up with Ryan. "Nothing that can't wait."

"Grab whatever you need and let's go."

Resigned to a few miserable hours, she put on her shoes, scooped up her purse and followed him out the door with a serious lack of enthusiasm weighting her steps. She'd rather spend her day staked to an ant hill than beside him in his Corvette.

His absolute certainty that he'd win custody of her baby unsettled her and made her doubt her ability to do her job. Her job was to give Beth and Patrick the family they yearned for.

He negotiated his way out of downtown and headed east on the interstate before glancing in her direction. "You left the house early this morning. I called at eight."

She wasn't in the mood for chitchat, but the situation demanded she keep things civil. When she caught herself studying the way his khaki pants clung to his long, muscular thighs she quickly transferred her attention to the rolling hills outside the windshield.

"There was an early-bird sale across town. Beth and I were shopping for baby things. She gets teary-eyed and chokes up when she handles the tiny clothes. I bet you don't do that."

A beat of silence passed. "I thought pregnant women were supposed to be the emotional ones."

"Maybe she's having sympathy pains. Studies show that some husbands have sympathy morning sickness. Apparently adoptive mothers-to-be can, too. Beth and I were always close." Sometimes too close. Sometimes she'd wondered if Beth were living vicariously through her, because her sister preferred to stay at home and read or watch movies then hear about Nicole's adventures later.

"If men appear to share morning sickness it's only because watching their wives heave makes them want to do the same."

She struggled with the juvenile urge to stick out her tongue at him. She knew Beth shared her roller-coaster emotional swings—swings which had grown worse for both of them since Ryan had exploded into their lives two weeks ago—

because she'd witnessed a few wild fluctuations. "You are a cynic."

"Not a cynic. A realist. I see things for what they are."

And he was bitter, too, from the sounds of it. "What do you know about pregnant women?"

"I spent nine months with my ex-wife."

Shock stilled her breath. That implied he had fathered a child before. "You said firstborn Patricks always took over the family firm. Why isn't this child?"

"She wasn't mine." The hard, flat words opened a Pandora's box of questions.

"I'm not following. She was your wife's child but not yours?"

A nerve twitched in his clenched jaw. "Yes. The neighborhood is a mile ahead on your left."

She'd spotted the signs for several Douglas Lake housing developments a few miles back, but location didn't interest her at the moment. His evasion did.

"We've proven you're fertile, so she obviously didn't need to use donor sperm. Was she involved with someone before you? No, wait.

You said you were with her for the full nine months. You're going to have to explain that."

He sliced a quick, hard glance her way. "And if I said it's none of your business?"

"I'd remind you you're the one who told me to ask questions about your sexual history."

He pursed his lips and blew out a slow breath. "My girlfriend was screwing my best friend. I was too blind to see it. When the pregnancy test turned up positive she swore the baby was mine. I married her. Turns out she lied."

Poor guy. From the sounds of it, like her father he'd been wronged by the woman he loved. But unlike her father, Ryan hadn't hung around for more of the same bad medicine. But then everyone knew her father only stayed because the money came from her mother's side of the family, and her mother owned the lion's share of Hightower Aviation.

"I'm sorry. How long ago was that?"

"Fourteen years."

"Were you involved in her pregnancy before you found out?"

"Every damned day. Through every doctor's

appointment, every time she hugged the toilet and every midnight craving."

No wonder he was such a jerk now. Betrayal could make you bitter—if you chose to let it. She'd chosen not to. Just as she'd chosen not to let sympathy soften her dislike of him.

"How did you find out? Did your wife eventually tell you?"

"Hell no. My best friend was African-American. Let's just say my beautiful blond wife's daughter was the spitting image of her daddy."

Ouch. So he'd lost a wife, a best friend and a child at the same time. Triple whammy. "Have you kept in touch with them?"

"Why would I?"

Typical male. "Is she happier with him than she was with you?"

"How the hell would I know? And why would I care?"

"If you truly love someone, then you want them to be happy—even if it's not with you." That's what she wished for Patrick.

Ryan looked at her as if she'd lost her mind. "That's bull."

"We choose whether to look on the positive or negative side of a situation."

"You're a real Pollyanna, aren't you?"

Her spine stiffened. Was he laughing at her? "Because I focus on what I have instead of what I don't have?"

Shaking his head, he turned the car into a new and exclusive waterfront community, went a few blocks then drove up a winding driveway through thick evergreen trees. The property had to be several acres. A beautiful two-story house with a wraparound porch came into view, but even before he stopped the car by the three-car garage Nicole knew the place would never work.

A multitude of objections gathered on her tongue, but "No," was all her quickly tiring brain could manage.

"You haven't even seen the place."

She smothered the yawn she couldn't hold back. "All I need to see is the steep drop-off to the lake. If you tripped, you'd roll like a snowball going down a ski slope. Don't get me wrong, Ryan, the house is gorgeous and it's a lovely neighborhood, but there's no way to make that yard safe for a toddler to run and play in."

He scanned the property again as if verifying her words.

"Wait here." He climbed from the car and greeted the suit-clad woman climbing from a minivan bearing a local real estate agent's sign on the door. After speaking with her he returned to the Corvette.

Resting his forearm on the steering wheel, he twisted in his seat to face her. "The next house is waterfront, too. Should we even bother to look at it?"

"You like your water, don't you?"

"I used to row and wakeboard competitively in college."

Why didn't that surprise her? He had the wide shoulders and thick biceps either of those sports would develop. One of those big arms drew her attention now. She'd bet the fingers of both her hands together couldn't circle the width. For a split second she wondered what he'd look like wearing nothing but swim trunks. Shaking her head, she banished the image of his lean, tanned frame.

Why did his physique fascinate her?

Because your child carries half his DNA and might inherit some of those attractive traits.

Satisfied with her answer she met his gaze. “Water is a hazard. But if you can fence it off, then maybe it would work. I guess this means you’re not going to give up your dangerous toys just because you’re about to become a father.”

His eyes narrowed. “No.”

She gave him credit for his honesty—even though she knew she’d recommend Beth to use it against him in the custody battle. But Ryan had a lot to learn if he thought a baby wouldn’t change his life. She wasn’t even keeping the child, and pregnancy had completely changed hers. She wasn’t sure her life would ever return to normal.

Five

Ryan couldn't remember the last time a woman had fallen asleep on him without the prelude of mind-blowing sex. The sleep part had always been his cue to slip out and avoid the postmortem. Leaving wasn't an option now.

Waiting for the red light to change, he silently drummed his fingers on the steering wheel and let his gaze skim over Nicole's face. Her thick lashes couldn't conceal the lavender circles beneath her eyes. According to her clinic file she was about ten weeks pregnant, in her first trimester.

Jeanette had slept a lot, too, during those early

weeks. She'd missed enough classes to flunk out of college. His ex had also complained incessantly about her lack of energy, her nausea and her frequent need to pee—as if each irritation had been Ryan's fault. She'd wanted to be waited on hand and foot and played every sympathy card in the deck. Love-struck sucker that he'd been he'd fallen for her act. His mother's manipulative attitude should have made him immune to those kinds of tricks, but the old "Love is blind" adage had certainly applied to him.

Nicole, on the other hand, hadn't said a word about her condition. She hadn't even complained about being hungry. She'd simply pulled a snack and a bottle of water from her tote bag. And then twenty minutes ago in the middle of discussing the pros and cons of the house they'd toured she'd trailed off midsentence. He'd looked over and found her slumped sideway in her seat asleep.

The tilted position caused her V-neck top to gape, revealing the swell of her pale breasts. That distracting sight combined with her soft, parted lips had hit him with a grenade of hunger.

The urge to stroke a silky lock of hair from her

cheek was about as welcome as a severe case of poison ivy. He shook off the feeling and focused on their earlier conversation. She was right about the water hazard. He couldn't be sure any nanny he hired would be diligent enough to never let the kid out of sight. That was one reason he appreciated Nicole's perspective. While he'd examined the structural integrity of the house she studied the practical aspects. Teamwork.

He checked his watch. He'd driven around for the past twenty minutes to let Nicole sleep, but now it was time to implement phase two of his plan. The light changed. He accelerated and turned toward the restaurant where he knew his father would be meeting his golf buddies later for the obligatory after-eighteen-holes cocktails.

After he snagged a parking space he killed the engine. As soon as the car fell silent Nicole's lids fluttered open. She sat up quickly, scanned her surroundings and touched her chin as if checking for drool. He found the insecure gesture oddly endearing. His lips twitched.

Those eyes hit him like laser beams, and he felt the heat and the pull deep in his gut. He took a mental giant step backward. The need to test the softness of her lips was damned hard to resist. If she weren't carrying his child, he'd act on this attraction, but the pregnancy was a complication. That didn't mean he wasn't tempted. He just had better sense. Having an affair plus sharing a child with her meant a continuing connection. He wasn't going there. This kid would be his and his alone, not leverage between parents. Once he had custody of the child he didn't intend to see her again.

Nicole smoothed her hair. "I'm sorry. I must have drifted off. Why are we here?"

"I made dinner reservations."

She blinked. "You're assuming I'll eat with you."

Her less than enthusiastic response took a bite out of his ego. He wasn't used to women refusing his company.

"I'm assuming you're hungry. Other than the squirrel food you pulled out of your purse over an hour ago, you've had nothing to eat all afternoon. In my experience pregnant women need to eat regularly."

"Dried fruit is a healthy snack."

"It wasn't substantial enough to keep a rodent going. Did you have other plans tonight?"

She glanced at the steak house, inhaled deeply and licked her lips. No doubt the aroma of grilling beef emanating from the premises made her mouth water as it did his. That was the only reason his mouth dampened. His reaction had nothing to do with the slow glide of her pink tongue. "No."

"Then let's eat. You can give me a list of things the agent needs to look for in the next house." He climbed from the vehicle and came around to her side. He reached her just in time to see her swing those long legs out the door. Her thigh and calf muscles flexed beneath the hem of her above-the-knee-length dress as she rose. She had great muscle tone, but she was lean like a distance biker or a runner.

He offered a hand which she ignored. Point taken. She didn't want this to feel like a date any more than he did. And while part of him respected the boundaries she marked, another part of him wanted an excuse for contact. But that would be flirting with danger. Not smart.

As he escorted her to the entrance he placed his palm at the base of her spine. Her startled jump let him know his touch wasn't welcome, and the tingle rising up his arm warned him that he danced on a hazardous edge.

Inside the darkened pub-style interior he gave the hostess his name. She led him and Nicole toward the table for two he'd requested. His gaze drifted past Nicole's slender waist to her slim hips in the burgundy dress. No one would guess her condition if she didn't tell them, and he was counting on her not volunteering the information in the next hour.

The waitress took their drink and appetizer orders and left them a basket of rolls. Nicole immediately selected a piece of bread, split it open and slathered butter on the steaming center. The hot yeasty smell reached across the table.

Her blissful expression as she tore off small pieces and tucked them between her lips made it look as if the bread were the most delicious thing she'd ever put in her mouth. For some reason that made him think of sex. Would she look the same when she took a man inside her?

He reached for his iced water, but clenching the cold glass didn't distract him. The woman was getting to him—probably a combination of knowing he couldn't have her and his recent celibacy. Since he'd begun his surrogate search he hadn't had time for a relationship. All the energy he hadn't devoted to his job had been expended on reaching his goal.

"You've shot down two houses. Do you have any suggestions for where to look next?"

"North Knoxville is nice."

Near her sister's suburban cookie-cutter neighborhood. Decent area, but a little too stifling for his tastes. "If I had time I'd design and build a house."

"Why don't you?"

He hoped the kid had her eyes. The color reminded him of the Caribbean waters off the bow of the sailing yacht he'd cruised on last summer. "Six months isn't long enough to do it right."

"If you used your surrogate you'd have more time."

The statement surprised a chuckle out of him. Persistent, wasn't she? He gave her credit for trying. "She's been paid for her time and released from her contract."

"I'm sure you could get her back if you wanted—"

"I don't."

She abandoned the last bite of bread. "Ryan, it would be easier for everyone if you let this go."

"The easy way isn't always the right way. And time is an issue. I want a baby before next summer." Before his father retired.

The front door swung open. His father and his buddies walked in right on time. Dear old Dad had a habit of scanning any room to search for potential connections. Ryan always did the same, but he hoped he was more subtle. As expected, his father spotted them and broke away from his group to stride in Ryan's direction.

He stopped by the table and, ignoring Ryan, offered his hand to Nicole with as much polish as a politician. "We haven't met. I'm Harlan Patrick. You're Nicole Hightower."

Nicole blinked and sent a quick questioning glance Ryan's way before pasting on a professional smile. "Yes. You're Ryan's father?"

She couldn't miss the resemblance. His father might be six inches shorter and twenty pounds heavier, but otherwise, they looked a lot alike. Same hair. Same eyes. Same profile. The Patrick Irish genes were strong.

"That's right. Ryan, you didn't tell me you were dining here tonight. You could have joined us."

"Nicole and I have business to discuss."

Ryan had chosen this table specifically because there wasn't any space for his father and his cronies to pull up another and join them. Nicole didn't seem like the type to blurt her condition to a stranger before she'd informed the rest of her family, but he didn't want to risk the news of her pregnancy slipping out and shocking the ultraconservative golfers—particularly his father who would definitely find fault with Ryan's method of providing an heir. After the fact was soon enough.

"Would you like to join us in the bar for a drink?" His father addressed Nicole.

"Nicole doesn't drink." Not while she was carrying his kid.

His father shot him a scowl. "I'd like to hear

more about Hightower Aviation. Patrick Architectural is considering engaging your services."

He noted his father didn't give him credit for the idea. He caught another flash of panic in Nicole's eyes. A pleat formed between her eyebrows before she turned back to his father. "I'm sure HAMC could meet your needs, but our sales department can answer your questions better than I can."

She dug in her purse, extracted a business card and pen and scribbled something on the back. "This is my brother Brent's direct line. Why don't you give him a call?"

Brent. The one who was probably cheating on his wife. After three minutes of his company at the picnic Ryan didn't like or trust the guy, and he didn't want him anywhere near his kid.

He took the card before his father could. "I've already spoken to one of your sales reps, Nicole, and given my father his card and a current brochure."

Nicole met his gaze. The color leeched from her face and a trapped look entered her eyes. "You didn't mention you'd been thinking of contracting our services."

"I've been investigating the possibility, and as I said, I've spoken to one of your salesmen. The idea is financially viable for us." He turned to his father. "Dad, if you'll excuse us?"

For some reason he was tired of sharing Nicole's company. The downward twitch of his father's lip told Ryan he didn't like being invited to leave, but after a moment Harlan nodded. "I'll talk to you later, Ryan. Nice meeting you, Ms. Hightower."

"You, too, sir." Her worry-filled eyes turned on Ryan as soon as his father was out of hearing range. "Why are you doing this?"

"This?"

"Intruding into my life."

"You have something I want. I'll stop at nothing to get it." And in this instance, winning was everything.

Darkness had fallen by the time Ryan paid the tab for dinner and escorted her from the steak house, increasing the sense of entrapment choking Nicole as they drove toward her home.

Ryan was crowding her and she didn't like it.

Her nails bit into her palms in the shadowy confines of his luxury sports car. "There are other airline management companies, you know. I could recommend a good one."

Ryan cut her a look, his face illuminated by the dashboard lights. "I've done my research. Hightower is the best. You have the largest staff and offer the widest selection of aircraft. HAMC has three global operating centers and a higher safety rating than any of your competitors. You provide services 24/7/365 on four hours' notice. The other companies can't compete."

All facts straight from the HAMC brochure, but hearing them from Ryan's lips turned the Cajun chicken pasta she'd eaten to lead in her stomach. If she couldn't talk him out of contracting HAMC, she'd be seeing him more often and that wasn't a good thing unless it gave her a link to her baby. But she'd prefer to get rid of that complication by getting rid of Ryan Patrick.

"Your Web page doesn't list any international projects. That makes one of the smaller companies more feasible and less expensive for you."

"Logistically it didn't make sense for us to

accept overseas jobs in the past because we do a lot of hands-on consulting after a project has begun. If we contract Hightower Aviation, we won't have to turn them down in the future."

Panic swelled inside her at the certainty in his voice. With any other man his confidence would have been attractive, but not so here. "Bigger isn't always better."

He kept his gaze on the road, but the amusement crinkling the corners of his eyes and carving a groove in his cheek told her he knew she was trying to run him off. "I'm surprised HAMC is still a privately owned company. Some corporate giant should have overtaken you by now."

She shrugged her stiff shoulders and realized he couldn't see the gesture. "Several have tried. My brother Trent is determined to prevent that from happening."

"You're financially strong and have a low debt to asset ratio. The odds are in your favor."

Her mouth went dry. "You've been checking up on us."

"I'd study any company I intended to indebt

Patrick Architectural a million plus dollars with over a five-year period."

Five years of seeing Ryan on a regular basis. She gulped.

She shouldn't be surprised by his diligence. From what she'd seen he wasn't stupid, just misguided and stubborn about the baby issue. "Still, a long-term commitment to a plane is a huge expense and a risky move in the current economic environment. You should be very, very sure before you contract our services."

"I'm sure—especially now that I'll have a child to rush home to. Less time on the road means more time with my kid."

The road to her personal hell was paved with his good intentions.

Her heart sank as she realized she might not be able to dissuade him from the custody battle.

He turned the car into her condo complex and parked in her driveway. She instantly reached for the door handle. "Thanks for dinner. But please call me before setting any more appointments to see houses. I do have other obligations."

"What could be more important than providing a safe home for this child?"

Nothing. She hated that he was right. She shoved open the door, bailed out and headed up the walk. The quiet thump of his soles echoing the rapid tap of her heels told her she hadn't escaped him. He followed her up the shallow stairs to her front door and crowded onto her tiny porch.

Her hanging baskets of petunias filled the humid evening air with their sweet smell, but they couldn't completely mask the subtle citrus tang of his cologne. It took her three tries to get the key into the lock. She twisted hard and fast and opened her door. Determined to get rid of him ASAP, she quickly stepped inside and turned abruptly to say goodbye. She collided with Ryan who had decided to follow her into her foyer despite the lack of invitation. The impact punched the air from her lungs and knocked her off balance.

Ryan grabbed her elbows to steady her. His pelvis, the length of his thighs and his chest pressed hers, scorching her. Her stomach did a funny flip-flop thing, then a spark of awareness flickered to life.

Nicole stared into his bright blue eyes, watching as Ryan's pupils expanded and his lips parted. The burn in her abdomen intensified and spread, warming and weighting her limbs. She couldn't get enough air through her nose and had to gulp deep breaths which only increased the pressure of his chest to her breast.

Back away, Nicole.

But she couldn't. Her muscles mutinied, refusing to take orders from her mind.

His gaze drifted to her mouth and panic pulsed through her. Surely he wasn't going to—His hands tightened and his head lowered, slowing down her brain. Transfixed she watched him come closer. Her heart raced and her breath hitched.

"Ryan, don't—"

His mouth smothered her protest. His lips were surprisingly soft, but at the same time commanding and hungry, plying hers with an expertise she couldn't help appreciating. She lifted her arms up to push him away, but her bullheaded fingers dug into his rock hard biceps and held on instead of shoving. Her muscles contracted, pulling him closer instead of pushing him away.

A shiver rippled through her like waves radiating from a stone thrown into a pond. His tongue stroked a molten trail across her bottom lip then penetrated, found hers and circled. A rush of desire shocked her, making her skin flush and her abdomen tighten.

She fought the heat spreading through her, and yet she couldn't dam the seeping awareness or make herself move away. How could she respond so intensely to Ryan—or any man for that matter—with the way she felt about Patrick? A sound meant to be a protest but sounding more like a moan slipped from her mouth into his, echoing in his low growl.

Ryan eased back incrementally, his grip loosening and the warmth of his body slowly leaving hers until only their lips clung. And then those, too, parted.

Gasping for air, Nicole pressed her fingers to her mouth and tried not to pant. "You shouldn't have done that."

"Agreed." His low, rough tone scraped over her exposed nerves like short nails on bare skin.

She hugged her arms around her middle and fought to stop the tremors that racked her. No man's kiss had ever rocked her that intensely. Not even Patrick's. She staggered back in her tiny foyer until her heels hit the bottom stair.

Why had Ryan's kiss packed such a punch? She searched her brain for a logical explanation for her illogical reaction and grasped on to the first idea that came to her.

"We're just drawn to each other because of our crazy situation. You're not my type. I don't want you."

His gaze dropped to her breasts. She didn't have to look down to know what he saw. Her nipples tingled, telling her they were tight and very likely tenting her blouse and contradicting her words. Damn her out-of-control hormones.

She'd read some pregnant women often craved sex, but she hadn't expected to experience the phenomenon. While she liked sex, it had never been one of those things she couldn't live without.

Ryan brushed her cheek with a fingertip. The

simple touch hit her like a crackling power line. "I don't want to want you, either, Nicole, but I find you very attractive."

Hearing the gravelly words only exacerbated the needy spasms of her internal muscles. She dodged out of reach on unsteady legs, stopping in the archway leading to her den. "Please don't say that or do that again."

He held her gaze without blinking. "I'm not making promises I'm not sure I can keep."

Her breath shuddered out, pounded out of her chest by her hammering heart. "You need to go."

"I'll call you when the real estate agent locates the next house."

She wanted to scream at him to never call again.

But she couldn't. Beth and Patrick were counting on her to keep the peace. Somehow, some way, she would not let them down.

"Way to go," Trent said as he entered Nicole's office Monday afternoon.

Her brother wasn't the type to offer approval unless something really big had happened.

"What are you talking about?"

"Patrick Architectural just bought fractional ownership in a Cessna Citation X. They listed you as the referral."

Not what she wanted to hear. But she'd been warned.

The Citation was the fastest midsize jet HAMC offered. She gave Ryan credit for going top-of-the-line. Her attention fell to the client file in Trent's hand. His arm lifted, extending across her desk and offering a burgundy-and-gold folder. The color combination signified a contract for the highest level of service HAMC provided.

Déjà vu. Another document she didn't want to read.

"They've requested you as their client aircraft manager."

Her stomach plunged as if she'd just parachuted from a plane—something she'd never do again because she hadn't enjoyed the being-out-of-control sensation. "Trent, my casebook is full. Please assign them another CAM."

"Not an option." His clipped tone warned her not to argue, but that wasn't going to stop her. Not this time. She had too much to lose.

"I really can't handle another client without my performance suffering on the ones I already have."

"I doubt that will be a problem, but if you're concerned we'll shift some of your other customers to someone else."

"No. I don't want to give up any of my people. They're like family." And like every family, hers had some eccentrics who required special handling.

His eyebrows dived toward his nose. "Tough. This deal was contingent on your acceptance."

She had to talk to Beth and get her sister to announce the pregnancy to the family. Until she did, Nicole couldn't explain to her brother why she had to refuse Patrick Architectural. How could she work with someone when she was about to become embroiled in a nasty custody battle over the baby she carried with him? But until then…

"C'mon, Trent, I never argue and never refuse an assignment—not even the most difficult cases that others have dumped. You know that. So the fact that I'm asking for a break now tells you I need it."

His face didn't soften one iota. "Let Becky know who you're handing over by the end of the day."

"You're pawning me off on your assistant? Trent—"

"Familiarize yourself with the file. Your first meeting with your new client is Friday afternoon, two o'clock."

"But—"

"There are no buts, Nicole. It's a done deal. Patrick Architectural is yours." He dropped the file on her desk, pivoted and stalked out.

Case closed. Nobody won an argument with her big brother—especially when he was locked in stubborn mode.

Nicole flopped back in her office chair and stared at the ceiling. This could not happen. And it had nothing to do with that kiss. Nothing. Absolutely, positively nothing.

Her lips tingled as if she could feel Ryan's kiss again, and that stirred up a termites' swarm in her belly. And termites left nothing but destruction in their path. She was very, very afraid Ryan might kiss her again, and that she'd do something stupid like her mother and act on that lust.

No, she wouldn't. The kiss had been a fluke, a combination of out-of-control pregnancy hormones and the strange tie she had with him as the father of her baby. That's all. She was certain of it.

Well…mostly certain.

She could call Ryan and plead conflict of interest, but she suspected her arguments would fall on deaf ears. He was tightening the screws and he'd show no mercy. That meant she had to talk to Beth. Now. She bolted to her feet, and ignoring a slight wave of dizziness, charged out of her office.

"Hey, where are you going?" Lea called out. "You have Tri-Tech in ten minutes."

Ten minutes. Normally she'd be at her desk reviewing the file ten minutes before a meeting. She couldn't today.

"Are you okay?"

"I have to talk to Beth. I should be back, but if I'm not, make sure Ronnie gets his coffee with cream and three spoons of sugar, and a raspberry jelly donut."

As the CAM in charge of each owner's service team she knew her client's preferences as well as she knew her own.

"Got it, boss." Lea snapped a smart-aleck salute.

Nicole didn't want to wait for the elevator or risk running into Ronnie coming up and have to return to her office before talking to her sister. She headed for the stairs and jogged down three flights. She was slightly winded and perspiration dampened her skin by the time she knocked on Beth's open door.

With the phone to her ear, Beth held up one finger, pointed at the visitor chair and turned away. But Nicole couldn't possibly sit still. She checked her watch. Eight minutes. She'd never been late for an appointment before and didn't want to start now. She prided herself on promptness.

What felt like an eon later but was actually only two minutes—she knew because she counted off the seconds—Beth cradled the receiver and faced her. "What's up?"

"We have to tell the family about the baby."

Beth stiffened. "Not yet."

"Beth, Ryan Patrick's company just contracted us and demanded me as their CAM. I can't do it. You and I know why, but I can't tell Trent the reason I must be excused until you let the family in on our little secret."

Beth bit her bottom lip, shifted in her seat and shook her head. "I'm not ready."

"What do you mean, you're not ready? I'll be showing soon."

Tense, silent seconds passed. "Nicole, Patrick and I are…having problems."

Nicole's heart stuttered. She knew they argued. "Every marriage has rough spots."

"This is bigger than that."

Her pulse fluttered. In the first few years of Beth and Patrick's marriage, Nicole had selfishly wished for Patrick to realize he'd married the wrong sister. But that wasn't what she wanted or needed now. If Beth and Patrick separated with Ryan circling like a shark, the custody issue would only get more complicated, and Ryan would stand a better chance of winning.

"Is it because the baby's not his?"

Beth adjusted the pens on her desk. "That's part of it."

A fresh wave of panic hit. What would she do if they decided not to adopt her baby? Ryan would win and she might never see her child again.

"You'll work it out, Beth. You've always

worked it out before. You guys are perfect for each other. Remember?" She heard the desperate edge to her voice.

"This time is different."

"I'll help. I'll talk to Patrick. I'll do whatever you need me to do, but you guys have to stay together. You love each other." The irony of begging for the man who possessed her heart to stay married to another woman didn't escape her.

"Nicole, sometimes love is not enough. And the timing for the announcement is all wrong."

"You've known for five weeks."

"Give me a little more time," Beth said with a tight smile. "And then everything will be settled."

Nicole pressed a hand over the little life causing so much upheaval and felt the extra firmness beneath the skin. "I don't have more time. And you know we're having the ultrasound Wednesday. You're going to want to share the pictures. The doctor even said she'd make a video of the baby for us."

"Patrick and I will have to watch the video later. I'm not ready to share the news."

Surprise rocked her back on her heels. "*Later?* You're not coming to the appointment?"

Beth made a show of checking her calendar. "I can't get away."

Nicole couldn't remember Beth ever lying to her before. Lying *for* her, sure. Many times. But she knew from the look in her sister's eyes Beth was telling a whopper this time. Beth was HAMC's publicist and there were no urgent marketing campaigns going on now. September was traditionally a slow month, and Beth's office was practically a tomb. It had been no big deal when Patrick and Beth had skipped the earlier routine appointments, but this time they'd get their first look at their future son or daughter.

Pain made Nicole look down. She'd dug nails so deeply into her palms she'd broken a fingernail at the quick. Blood filled the tiny crack. That was going to hurt for a while.

But not as long as losing her baby would.

Her thoughts swirled like leaves in a windstorm. Needing to collect herself, she checked her watch and realized she was out of time. Panic rose within her.

"Beth. Please reconsider. I can't keep Ryan on my client roster."

"I'm sorry, Nicole, but we can't make the announcement yet. Maybe in a few weeks."

A few weeks. Two weeks ago Beth had barely been able to contain the news, then at the picnic she'd begged for a few more days. And now she was delaying *weeks?*

Nicole had a bad feeling about the whole situation. Something was really, really wrong, and until she knew what it was, she couldn't fix it.

"Beth, I need your help."

"This isn't high school anymore, Nicole. It's not as simple as lying for you like I did when you skipped class or picking you up when your date dumped you on the side of the road because you refused to put out, or forging Mom's signature on a note home from your teacher. Handle your own damned problems for once and quit screaming for me."

Stunned speechless by Beth's vehemence, Nicole fisted her cold fingers by her side. She was on her own and she had no idea how to handle the disaster that had become her life.

Six

The back of Nicole's neck prickled late Wednesday morning. On alert, she swiveled her office chair away from her side desk. Ryan leaned against the doorjamb and observed her through narrowed eyes. Her heart slammed against her rib cage.

"Ryan Patrick to see you," Lea chirped from beside him.

Nicole cut her assistant a dry look and caught the matchmaking glint in her eyes. "I can see that."

Lea grinned unrepentantly and shrugged. "Sorry, I was stuck on the phone and I waved him through. I knew you were only finishing the pilot scheduling chart."

How long had Ryan been watching her? Had she done anything obnoxious?

"Thank you, Lea." Nicole didn't want to talk to him, but while she could get away with refusing personal visits at work, she couldn't refuse to see a client, and she didn't know in which capacity he'd come today. Judging from his tailored gray suit he'd come from work. He looked handsome, successful and rich like so many of the other HAMC clients, but her reaction to him was far from her usual business-only response. He had a way of looking at her that made her feel jumpy, jittery, tongue-tied and feminine.

Pressing suddenly damp palms to her skirt, she rose. "Good morning, Ryan. I wasn't expecting you until Friday."

It took a conscious effort to keep her gaze from drifting to his mouth, but that didn't keep her lips from warming at the memory of a kiss she couldn't seem to erase no matter how hard she tried.

"The agent has two houses lined up on this

side of town. Ride over with me during your lunch hour."

An order. Not an invitation. His timing couldn't be worse.

Lea practically jumped for joy. "You're looking at houses together?"

Nicole winced. "I'm helping Ryan find a place for himself."

Lea's face fell. "Oh, I thought maybe you two—"

"Lea, don't you have supplies to order for an overseas flight?"

Behind Ryan's back Lea stuck out her tongue. Nicole ignored her and glanced at her watch. "If you'd called, I would have told you I can't go with you. I already have something scheduled, and I have to leave in a moment."

Ryan had insisted on being present at each doctor's appointment. Should she tell him where she was going?

No.

And then she remembered Lea knew. But Lea didn't know the baby was Ryan's. Nicole hadn't dropped that bomb yet. But surely her assistant wouldn't—

"I want to see the ultrasound video of the little tadpole when you get back," Lea said. "You said the doctor was going to record it on a CD, right?"

Nicole's body went cold. She simultaneously wanted to dive beneath her desk and strangle Lea. She prayed Ryan wouldn't understand the remark. "We'll discuss that *later.*"

Ryan straightened and his alert blue gaze probed hers. "You have a doctor's appointment today?"

So much for keeping secrets. She swallowed. "Yes."

"You didn't tell me."

"No."

Out of the corner of her eye she caught Lea's frown as if her assistant had finally picked up on the undercurrents. "Lea, please excuse us."

Lea didn't move. Ryan cut her a look and she backed out of the room. He shut the door in her face. "I told you I expected to be included in any doctor's visits."

"My attorney says I don't have to let you into

my private appointments. You're entitled to the doctor's notes pertaining to the baby and that's it."

Without moving a muscle, his demeanor changed completely. He suddenly looked dark, dangerous and fierce, his eyes glinting like ice chips and his face rigid. Not the kind of guy you'd want to meet in a dark alley.

"You don't want to start a war with me, Nicole." The quietly uttered words packed more punch than if he'd shouted them.

No, she didn't want to fight with him and not only because her attorney had cautioned Nicole against causing unnecessary friction. Okay, she might as well admit that if not for the baby, she'd enjoy Ryan's company. He was smart, attractive and ambitious—all the things she enjoyed in a date. But none of that mattered since she wasn't looking for a relationship.

She licked her dry lips. "I'll burn you a copy of the ultrasound video."

"Not good enough. I want to be there where I can ask questions."

While she understood his request and admired his dedication to his child, she suspected she'd be an emotional wreck during and after this appointment. Agreeing to have a child and give it away was one thing. Actually seeing the baby growing inside her and knowing it was a part of her and yet it wasn't hers was another. She didn't want Ryan to witness any potential meltdown she might have.

She shook her head. "I'm sorry. I really need to do this alone."

"Not an option."

That made twice this week she'd heard that phrase. She liked it even less this time. "Ryan—"

"I'm coming with you."

"What about the houses?"

"I'll postpone our appointment."

She could object to him shadowing her, call her lawyer and put the legal wheels in motion to stop Ryan from butting in, but as her attorney had pointed out, a nationally acclaimed fertility clinic's mix-up between two prominent Knoxville families was the kind of fodder tabloids loved to exploit. She'd lose credibility with her clients if that happened. And considering her family didn't even know about the pregnancy yet, exposure through the media wasn't a path Nicole wanted to take. Besides, hadn't her mother's affairs garnered enough bad publicity for Hightower Aviation?

The alarm on her cell phone chimed. If she didn't leave now she'd be late for her appointment. Being late or taking legal action meant rescheduling, and she didn't want to wait even one more day to see her—*Beth's* baby. She shut off the alarm.

Letting Ryan accompany her was the most expedient choice. Even if she hated it. She sighed in defeat. "You can follow me to the medical complex in your car."

"And give you the chance to lose me in traffic? No. We'll ride together." He withdrew his key ring from his pocket.

Her hackles rose. He might have her backed into a corner, but that didn't mean she had to go down without a fight. "I'm driving."

With a shrug he pocketed his keys and opened the door then extended his arm, palm up, to indicate she lead the way. Nicole snatched her purse out of the drawer and marched ahead. His palm pressed her lower back and her pulse jumped. She wished he'd quit doing that—at least until she could numb herself to his touch.

Thank goodness Lea was on the phone, but her eyes rounded as she took in Nicole leaving with Ryan and the familiar placement of his hand. There would be questions later, and eventually Nicole would have to figure out how much she was going to share. Right now she was too rattled to worry about it.

She led the way to her car. Ryan folded himself into the passenger seat. "Nice ride."

Her pearl-white Cadillac SRX Crossover was both comfortable and roomy. "I have to taxi clients and their luggage around sometimes. As you may have guessed, we deal with high-end clientele. A luxurious vehicle is a necessity."

He turned off her stereo, silencing the soothing flute concerto playing quietly in the background. "Are Beth and Patrick meeting us at the doctor's?"

Ryan didn't need to know about the dissension between Beth and Patrick. Nicole pointed the car toward the medical complex and tried to come up with an answer that wouldn't lead to more questions. She couldn't. "No."

"Aren't they interested in the kid?"

"Yes. But they're…today's not a good day."

His lips and eyes narrowed. "For either of them?"

"No. They'll watch the video."

Ryan's presence overpowered the interior of her car. She'd never felt this cramped even with four clients packed inside and had never been as conscious of anyone's scent as she was the subtle hint of his cologne.

Her gaze strayed to the tanned, long-fingered hands resting on his thighs. How would those hands feel on her skin? Her stomach swooped at the taboo question. She shut down that line of thinking…or tried to, but her out-of-whack hormones wouldn't let her.

"Ryan, I can't be your CAM. It's a conflict of interest."

"One your brother assured me you'd make work."

"You told him about the baby?" Her voice squeaked.

"No. I told him we were…acquainted. He drew his own conclusions."

"You mean he thinks we're lovers." She shot

him an exasperated look. "Torturing me is not going to make this go any smoother."

"I'm not torturing you. I'm going after what's mine."

"I keep telling you. The baby isn't yours except by a genetic link. You have no more connection to it than any other sperm donor does to his offspring."

"I have a legal connection. That's what matters."

She wasn't going to win this war of words. The brick office building came into view. Every muscle in her body snapped taut. The ultrasound was going to be hard. Part of her ached to see the life growing inside her. Part of her dreaded it. She parked, but her hands couldn't seem to release the steering wheel.

"Nicole?"

"We're here," she said in as cheerful a voice as she could muster. When his frown deepened she wanted the stupid, unnecessary words back, but she couldn't unsay them, so she met Ryan's gaze and tried to emit a calm vibe. From his serious expression she'd guess she received a D minus for her effort.

"Is this your first ultrasound?"

Her fingers remained clenched. Her knuckles looked blanched in the sunlight. "Yes."

"Let's do it." He shoved open his door, exited the car and came around to open her door. When she didn't get out, he crouched down to meet her at eye level. "The scan won't hurt you or the baby. You have nothing to worry about."

Surprise jerked her eyes to his. *He* was comforting *her?* "I know it won't hurt."

He offered a hand. "Come on. Let's go see what we've made."

She almost liked him at that moment.

She willed her muscles to loosen and accepted his assistance. His warm fingers closed around hers and tugged her from the car. She found the contact calming which was exactly why she pulled free. She couldn't afford to lean on him or to trust him. Her legs quivered with each step as she accompanied him to the building, and her voice shook as she gave the receptionist her name.

She sat in a vinyl chair beside Ryan and scanned the room. Several women smiled at him then at her as if they believed them to be a happy, expectant couple. She wanted to correct them. But she didn't. She noted the rounded tummies of the moms-to-be. That would be her in a matter of months. On the other side of the room a tiny baby slept in a carrier beside a woman who looked both exhausted and exhilarated.

That would not be her. When she came for her postpartum checkup she would be alone. And empty. Her baby wouldn't be hers anymore.

It's not yours now.

Her chest ached and her throat tightened. An urge to run raced through her, and a choked sound bubbled from her throat. She tried to cover it by faking a cough.

Ryan's hand covered hers on the armrest. Startled, she lifted her gaze and found understanding in his eyes. Her breath caught. How could he possibly know how much this hurt? She shifted her hand to her lap. She didn't want to share her misery with him. It left her feeling exposed and vulnerable.

"Nicole?" a pink-scrub-clad woman called from the door to the treatment rooms. Nicole bolted to her feet and raced away from the unwanted connection she felt with him.

Ryan shadowed her steps.

"Who do we have with us today?" the woman asked with a sunny smile.

"Ryan Patrick, the baby's father," Ryan said before Nicole could find the words to explain their convoluted relationship.

"You're going to see your little one today," Ms. Cheerful said as she waved Nicole onto the scale. "But first… Let's see how Mommy is doing."

Mommy. Nicole's throat closed up. No, she wouldn't be a mommy.

The nurse noted Nicole's weight and took her blood pressure. "Any problems? Are you keeping food down okay? Having regular bowel movements?"

Nicole's cheeks burned. Including Ryan in such a personal conversation seemed…invasive. "I'm fine. Everything's fine."

"Dad and I will wait for you in room four. You head off to the lab."

Dad.

Nicole's gaze jerked to Ryan's. He looked a

little shell-shocked. Good. She shouldn't be the only one suffering here.

She ducked into the lab and let the technician do her thing, wondering all the while what Ryan was telling the nurse. Nicole headed to the exam room as soon as she could.

"First babies are always the most exciting," the nurse was saying as Nicole entered. "And it's early, but you might possibly get a peek at the sex today. Do you want to know?"

"No," Nicole blurted.

"Yes," Ryan answered simultaneously.

The nurse chuckled. "I'll warn the doctor we have a difference of opinion."

Understatement of the year.

As far as Nicole was concerned, the less she knew about the baby the less she'd bond with it before she had to relinquish.

The nurse laid a folded pink paper sheet on the table. "Dr. Lewis will be right in. Strip off the skirt, sweetie, and cover your lower half with this."

Nicole froze. The nurse left before she could protest. Nicole's breath burned in her chest and her heart thundered like stampeding horses as she slowly lifted her gaze to Ryan's. She couldn't help cringing when she remembered the underwear she'd put on today. The scrap of black lace was practically nonexistent, but the woman at the appointment desk last time had suggested Nicole go tiny or bare for the ultrasound.

Ryan did not need to see her in her underwear.

She gulped then she noticed the curtain tucked out of the way in the corner. A yank sent it sailing along the track on the ceiling, separating her from those intrusive blue eyes. But even though she couldn't see him, she knew he was there on the other side of the thin floral fabric. Her hands shook so badly she could barely unfasten her skirt. She was beginning to think she'd have to ask for help in manipulating the button at her lower back when it popped free.

With a sigh of relief she checked to be sure the curtain was still in place, stepped out of the garment and draped it over a chair. She snatched up the pink sheet, unfolded it and wrapped it around her lower half. The protective paper sheet covering the vinyl made a god-awful racket as she climbed on the exam table and sat. She double- and then triple-checked to make sure she had everything concealed that could be hidden from Ryan's prying eyes.

The door to the hall opened. "Well hello," the doctor's voice greeted Ryan. "And you are?"

"Ryan Patrick. The baby's father."

"I'm Debbie Lewis, Nicole's OB. Nicole didn't tell me you'd be joining us today."

"I'll be here for every appointment."

Ryan's answer made Nicole shudder. She gave her doctor points for taking Ryan's presence in stride. Debbie knew the basic situation, but she didn't let on that having Ryan here was anything out of the ordinary.

Debbie peeked around the edge of the curtain. "Hello, Nicole. Are you ready for this?"

No. "Yes."

Debbie whipped the curtain back to the corner. "Lay back."

Nicole did as asked, the paper crinkling noisily. But she couldn't care less about the paper beneath her. She was more concerned with anchoring the slipping pink sheet, and Ryan standing a few feet away and watching her every move.

"Lift your top for me," Debbie instructed.

Nicole focused on a seam in the wallpaper and hiked her camisole and sweater to her rib cage. She thought she heard Ryan inhale, but she was probably wrong. Cool air brushed her stomach from the air-conditioning gusting through the overhead vent.

The doctor tucked the pink sheet into the lace band of Nicole's panties then palpated her abdomen. After she took a few measurements and wrote them down she picked up a tube. "First we'll listen for the heartbeat with the Doppler. Brace yourself. The gel is cold."

Nicole winced when the chilly goo hit her skin. Determined to pretend Ryan wasn't there, she focused on the mobile spinning slowly above her. But she knew he was watching, looking at her pale who-has-time-to-tan? belly. She felt completely naked and exposed. But strangely, it wasn't a creepy feeling. An odd awareness crept over her, quickening her pulse, warming her skin and tightening her nipples. She wanted to cover them, but couldn't without being obvious.

Excitement about the baby. That's all it is.

You're about to hear and see the life growing inside you. It has nothing to do with Ryan.

The OB slid the small handheld instrument across Nicole's stomach just above her bikini line. The speaker emitted what first sounded like white noise then morphed into a rhythmic swishing pattern.

"That's your baby's heartbeat."

Nicole couldn't breathe. Against her will her gaze slid to Ryan's face. His brilliant blue stare focused on her stomach, and his throat worked as if he'd swallowed. His emotional response multiplied hers. Tears burned her throat and eyes.

Her baby's heartbeat.

No. Not yours.

Beth's. And Patrick's.

And Ryan's.

She was the only one left out of this equation.

Seven

H*is baby.*

It took one hundred percent of Ryan's concentration to force air into his deflated lungs.

The doctor pulled the device from Nicole's smooth ivory skin. He caught a glimpse of a sliver of black lace and brown curls a shade darker than the silky honey-toned hair on her head before the doctor adjusted the paper-thin pink sheet. Ryan clenched his teeth tighter. Nicole's toes curled, drawing his attention to her toenails which she'd painted a dusky shade of peach. The one-two punch of shock and arousal nearly knocked him off his feet. He sank into the visitor chair.

"The heart rate is approximately one hundred-sixty beats per minute. For a fetus at this stage it's in the normal range." The doctor wrote in the chart. Ryan struggled to pull himself together while she tugged a boxy apparatus with a TV screen on it from the corner and played with the knobs.

She squirted more clear gel on Nicole's belly and Nicole flinched. Goose bumps lifted her flesh. Ryan's fingers itched to test the texture, to warm her with his hands.

The doc followed the same procedure she'd used with the previous instrument, scrolling it below Nicole's navel until a ghostly image appeared on the screen.

"Here's our baby," she said.

The hairs on the back of Ryan's neck rose. He'd done this before, seen a baby he'd thought was his via ultrasound. He'd held Jeanette's hand, shared the excitement with her and soaked up every detail while planning to be the best parent he could possibly be. Only that opportunity and his heart had been ripped away from him.

Ryan tried to pull back, but he couldn't look away. He tried to maintain an objective attitude and keep his emotions out of the mix. This time he had three people determined to take this kid from him.

The doctor pointed to a lopsided circle that contracted and expanded like a fuzzy strobe light. "That's the heart."

His body went numb. His thoughts raced. He'd paddled the Yukon, parachuted from a plane, sailed the Bermuda Triangle and raced his Agusta motorcycle through the hairpin turns of Tail of the Dragon, but none of those feats gave him half the adrenaline rush of seeing that white, chalky form and that little pulsing blob.

The doctor shifted her cursor and clicked on the image. "This is the head. I'm going to take a few measurements. Right now your baby is only a few inches long, but the basic skeletal parts are recognizable. Can you see them?"

He could, but he couldn't find his voice. A nod was all he could manage. Ryan saw eyes, a nose, a little chin, and his throat closed up. The doctor pointed out the spine, the arms and legs and electronically measured each.

The chalky figure moved its hand and suddenly the picture in front of him became all too real. A little person with knees, elbows, fingers and toes.

His kid. *His.*

"Does the baby look healthy?" He sounded as if he had laryngitis.

"We can't see everything with ultrasound, but what I can see looks exactly the way it should."

The words didn't alleviate his gut-twisting tension. He told himself this was no different than construction. He was used to seeing sketches and blueprints of buildings yet to be built. Feeling the excitement and anticipation of pulling a project together and watching it develop from the ground up was nothing new. But he experienced that rush tenfold now along with a heart-pounding, lung-crushing shot of fear. In a few months this finished product would be his responsibility. But a child wasn't something he could make adjustments to if the wiring or plumbing didn't work out as expected.

A weird feeling crept over him. It was as if this event was happening to someone else or he was sitting in front of a Discovery Channel TV program. Detached, but engrossed. Awed. Mesmerized. This wasn't just a game of one-upmanship anymore or a case of winning or losing. This was life or death. And that little life was his responsibility. His. He'd do anything to protect it.

In theory, having an heir to insure his father would entrust the family firm to him had been a good plan. The reality of being held accountable for that child's well-being scared the crap out of him.

He pried his gaze from the shadowy image and looked at Nicole. Equal parts wonder and agony chased across her face, but the tears streaming from her eyes and dampening the pillow under her head as she stared at the screen without blinking hit him like a falling I beam.

He'd completely misread her. He'd believed having this baby for her sister and walking away was going to be easy for her. Wrong. Judging by the pain on her face she might well change her mind and refuse to relinquish.

He'd have to alter his strategy, because Nicole's greedy brother-in-law wasn't the weakest link. Nicole was. She was the one who could snatch his child from him at the last possible second—just like Jeanette had before.

If he wanted this baby, then Nicole Hightower was the one he had to work on, the one he had to win over.

To do that he needed to get closer to her. He had to get into her head so he could anticipate her next move and be prepared to counter it.

He wasn't losing another baby.

Nicole hurried from the building, running from her thoughts, running from her doubts and trying to escape the pain tearing her apart. Maternal instincts she hadn't known she possessed surged though her, making her desperate to flee her current situation.

How was she going to keep her promise to Beth and Patrick?

Unless they pulled out of the contract, she had to or she'd turn her family against her. Hurting Beth meant incurring the entire family's wrath. Beth might be her older sister, but she was also the acting matriarch of the family because their mother had abdicated that position a long time ago. At fifty-eight Jacqueline Hightower was little more than a figurehead president of the HAMC board of directors who wanted what she wanted and more often than not managed to get it.

Nicole knew giving Beth and Patrick the baby they'd wanted for so long was the right thing to do. She knew deep in her heart somewhere that once the stress of being denied the child they'd craved passed they'd be happy again.

But knowing that didn't lessen the ache in her chest.

You'll get past your doubts. Today was just a shock, that's all.

Ryan caught her elbow outside the doctor's office and pulled her to a stop yards short of her car. Despite the sun overhead, she was so cold she couldn't stop shivering. His hands buffed her biceps, warming her cold flesh through her sweater. She wished he'd quit touching her. The contact confused her.

Correction. Her reaction to his touch confused her.

Her shivering lessened. His hands stilled, squeezed in silent support that made her eyes burn with the few tears she hadn't shed all over the exam table. This was so much harder than she'd thought it would be. She struggled to mask the hurricane of emotions churning inside her before she lifted her face to his.

"Hand over the keys, Nicole." His voice was soft, gentle, and yet still commanding. His eyes held both sympathy and understanding. And then she remembered. He, too, knew how it felt to lose a child. He'd already been down the road she was about to travel. "You're in no shape to drive."

How astute of him to notice. She considered arguing, but she didn't have the energy. And he was right. She had no business behind the wheel at the moment. Uncurling her fist, she offered the keys. His short nails scraped her palm as he scooped her key ring from her hand, and a flaming arrow of energy shot up her arm and crash-landed in the pit of her stomach.

How did he do that? How did this man she barely knew affect her on such a visceral level? And when she was already an emotional waste-land? It couldn't be anything but the baby they shared. Her body must somehow recognize him as the father of her child on a primitive level.

He gently thumbed away a fresh tear then helped her into the car as if she were fragile, and circled to the driver's side.

No doubt about it, Ryan Patrick puzzled her. He was understanding and yet ruthless. He opened doors, held chairs, seated her before seating himself and did a multitude of other gestures you usually only saw from an older generation. And yet he went to a fertility clinic and hired a surrogate to have his baby.

The contradiction between his old-fashioned courtesies and his modern science choices intrigued her. And the emotional response to the baby that he hadn't been able to hide had shaken her conviction that he'd be a bad father. He'd been as enthralled by the image on the screen as she had. At that moment he'd become more than the man who wanted to take her baby. He'd become the father of the child she carried, someone with a valid emotional stake in the outcome of her pregnancy, someone with something precious to lose.

Someone like her.

But how could someone who always chased thrills be a good parent? Her parents were perfect examples. They'd traveled the globe, always searching for their next good time. Her mother chose men, her father casinos. And they'd left their children at home in the care of nannies. There had been some good, loving nannies who Nicole had hated to see go, but the majority had been there for the paycheck and even a child could feel the difference. Nicole had learned early on not to bond with someone who might leave unexpectedly.

Ryan slid into the driver's seat and turned the key. "What time is your next appointment?"

"I don't have any official appointments this afternoon. I'm working on scheduling and client special requests." She'd deliberately allowed for emotional recovery time after her doctor's visit and chasing down obscure items seemed like a good way to keep her mind from straying along forbidden paths. "Why?"

"We're having lunch before I take you back to work."

She'd planned to eat before returning to the

office, but not with him. She needed solitude to get her head together. "That's really not necessary."

"We both need the decompression time. We'll also pick up your prescription."

Hadn't he heard a word she said? "I can do that myself."

"I want to make sure you have it, and I intend to help you with your medical expenses."

Why? Because he genuinely wanted to help? Or because helping would give him leverage? "Thank you, but no."

"Are Beth and Patrick covering your medical bills?"

Another sore subject. "No. This is my gift to them. My health insurance covers almost everything."

"What kind of deal is that? You're making all the concessions."

"That's the way I want it." Beth had told her finances had been severely stretched by years' worth of failed fertility treatments.

"I don't want you cutting corners. I'm helping. Deal with it."

She did not need his bossy attitude right now.

She needed peace and quiet and time to think. The emotional appointment had drained her. Exhaustion made her head and shoulders heavy and her patience short. A tension headache nagged at her nape.

"Are you going to show up each morning to make sure I take the iron tablets along with my prenatal vitamins, too?"

Oops. So much for patience, politeness and perseverance. Sarcasm wasn't a good choice if she wanted to keep this on a friendly footing as her attorney had suggested.

"Do I need to?"

She didn't doubt he would for one minute. "I would never do anything to endanger my child."

"Our child. Yours and mine." His possessive tone sent a wave of goose bumps rolling across her skin. "Admit it, Nicole. After seeing the scan you don't want to give your sister and brother-in-law this baby."

The truth of his statement punched the air from her lungs. How had he known what she'd been unwilling to admit even to herself? Ryan read her too easily.

"What I want is irrelevant. I gave my word and signed a contract. The baby will be better off with two parents."

"Two parents who bicker incessantly?"

She smothered a wince. She'd hoped he'd missed that at the barbecue. "It's a high-stress time for Beth and Patrick. They've been trying to get pregnant for years. They love each other. It's just a little hard to see that right now. Once the baby arrives everything will be fine again."

"You don't honestly believe that?" His tone said he didn't.

After her conversation with Beth she wasn't as certain as she'd once been. Ryan didn't need to know that. "Yes, I do."

Ryan scowled harder. "It's better to be with a single parent who wants you than stuck between two who use you as a weapon against the other. I lived that life. My kid won't."

Sympathy and empathy she didn't want to feel for him invaded her like a rising tide. When her parents had fought she'd either taken cover or looked for a way to distract them. Distracting them more often than not meant she'd ended up in trouble—trouble Beth had had to fix when their parents had thrown their hands up in disgust. But at least it had stopped their fighting.

"I'm sorry, Ryan."

He shrugged. "I survived."

He turned into the closest restaurant driveway and pulled up to the drive-through speaker, cutting off her questions. Without asking her preference, he ordered a variety of foods. When they reached the window he handed her the massive bag. The mouthwatering aromas of fried chicken, barbecue, Brunswick stew and peach cobbler filled the car as he headed toward downtown, and at the moment she craved every fat-laden, Southern cooking calorie of those comfort foods.

Leaning back in her seat, she closed her eyes and held on to the hot bag. She'd counted ten fingers and ten toes on that black-and-white screen, and seeing those little digits wiggle had reached right out and grabbed her heart with crushing force.

How would she survive giving away her baby?

She didn't protest when Ryan drove into his

condo complex, but she bolted upright in her seat when he bypassed the building and pulled up to the dock. "Why are we here?"

"We're going to take a short boat ride and picnic."

Her uneasiness increased. "I don't think that's a good idea."

"Do you get motion sickness?"

That was the least of her worries. She didn't want to run the risk of another one of those misguided kisses when she hadn't been able to erase the first one from her mind. She was already vulnerable and that spark of attraction each time their fingers touched made it clear the earlier chemistry hadn't been a fluke.

Ryan made her feel things she shouldn't and didn't want to experience ever again. Things she didn't want to believe she was capable of feeling for any man other than Patrick. If she could experience that attraction for other men that would mean that there was some of her mother in her, and she didn't want to be like her fickle, promiscuous mother.

"I don't get seasick, but I can't waste a day on the river."

"Racing across the water with the wind in your hair will blow away the stress. The bike does the same thing on the road, but I'm not putting you on a motorcycle when you're pregnant."

Her older brothers had taught her to never admit weakness unless you wanted it to be used against you. "Who says I'm stressed? And just for the record, I don't want to ride your death rocket."

Ryan hit her with a lowered eyebrow look. "Riding a bike is only dangerous if you're careless. I'm not."

The conviction in his eyes told her he believed what he said.

He climbed from the car and paused beside the open door to remove his suit coat and toss it into the backseat. One tanned hand reached for his tie, loosening the knot and pulling the silk free. He released the cuffs of his shirt and then unbuttoned the placket.

Nicole shouldn't have been hypnotized by his actions, but she couldn't look away. Nor could she force herself into motion. For pity's sake, he wasn't going to get naked, but his movements were every bit as erotic as a slow striptease, and the show sent a surge of energy through her like she'd never before experienced.

Her exhaustion vanished, and tension fisted beneath her navel as he peeled off the dress shirt to reveal a snug white T-shirt underneath. The cotton molded his muscular chest and his pectorals as he braced himself on the roof with one arm and leaned in to lay his shirt and tie on top of his coat. Shadows of the dark whorls of his chest hair and the tiny beads of his nipples showed through the thin fabric.

Should she play it safe and insist he take her back to the office, or could she count on her usual aplomb to get her through this meal? Her stomach rumbled, giving her an answer—just not the one she wanted. She didn't want to spend time with him, but she'd be wise to take advantage of the opportunity she'd been presented, learn everything she could about him and find any weaknesses Beth and Patrick might use against him in a custody battle.

Resigned to her fate, she shoved open her door and hauled herself and the food out of the car before he reached her side. He took the bag from her.

"You'll be more comfortable without the sweater."

She glanced down at the black silk tie-waist cardigan she'd thrown over her burgundy camisole this morning when there'd been a slight chill in the air. The sun shone down from a blue cloudless sky, warming her skin, and a gentle breeze teased her hair, tugging strands free from her clip and blowing them across her face. She smoothed her hair back but bits slipped free again. It was a beautiful day, one of the few warm ones left before fall's frost nipped the air. Why not enjoy it?

She removed her sweater and dropped it on the car seat. Ryan pivoted and strode down the sidewalk toward the bobbing boats, his long, athletic stride eating up the distance.

Determined to eat quickly and get back to work, she followed him. He boarded a fast-looking white boat with a red racing stripe, set down the bag and then turned and held out his hand. "Pass me your shoes."

Second thoughts about spending the next hour on the water with him intruded, but she nonetheless removed her high-heeled pumps and gave them to him. He tucked her shoes in a side cubbyhole and once more offered assistance. "Come aboard."

Touching him again was a bad idea, but slipping might hurt the baby. She reluctantly laid her palm in his. Her body instantly responded with unwelcome enthusiasm to his heat and strength, and she had to fight the knee-jerk reaction to yank away. The boat rocked beneath her feet, but Ryan held her steady.

He pointed to the seat curving around the back of the craft. "Sit and relax. I'll get us underway."

She was too wound up to sit and there wasn't enough room to pace, so she stood, her toes digging into the short, thick, red carpet. But as she watched him move about the boat she couldn't help wondering if her child would inherit his athletic grace, his power. Would he or she grow up learning Ryan's old-fashioned courtly gestures?

Not if Patrick raises him.

The words dive-bombed her brain like an

annoying mosquito. She swatted them away. Patrick was the best father for her child. He was gentle and kind and patient, an intellectual with a love for learning. If he never opened doors or held chairs for her or her sister, it was because he was a modern man who treated women as equals.

He's henpecked.

The errant ugly thought startled her. Where had that come from? Sure Beth was bossy and liked to have her own way, and Patrick let her, but only because he loved her and didn't like to cause friction. His easygoing personality had been one of the things that had attracted Nicole to him in college. He'd been her raft in a stormy sea. Ryan was more like the storm itself, blowing in and wreaking havoc in her life. Patrick calmed her. Ryan confused and agitated her.

Ryan bent over the bow to cast off a rope. Her gaze roamed over his tight backside and down the firm flex of his hamstrings. His thick biceps and the breadth of his shoulders caught her attention. Attitude wasn't the only difference between her brother-in-law and the father of her baby.

Patrick was lean and wiry and couldn't be

called athletic by any stretch of the imagination. His movements were abrupt, and his clothes tended to hang on his frame rather than accentuate the shift of powerful muscles the way Ryan's T-shirt did.

Patrick reminded her of a hummingbird, all zip, dash, skittish and adorable, whereas Ryan was more like the hawk gliding purposefully over the bend in the river. Predatory. Determined. Persistent.

Ryan turned unexpectedly. Nicole yanked her eyes up to his a second too late. Her cheeks burned with guilt at being caught ogling his body.

He slowly straightened, his pupils dilating as he held her gaze. His nostrils flared. The memory of that taboo kiss made her mouth water and her pulse flutter wildly. She caught herself studying the chiseled shape of his upper lip and struggled to pull air into her tight lungs.

With tremendous effort, she pried her eyes away from temptation and focused on the big *T* on the side of Neyland Stadium, home of the Tennessee Volunteers. But the change in scenery did nothing to alleviate the awareness unfurling inside her like a morning glory seeking the sun. She silently screamed denial, but couldn't refute the truth.

She was sexually attracted to Ryan Patrick.

This can't happen. Not with him.

She felt each step he took on the boat deck through the soles of her feet, and she saw him approach in her peripheral vision. Her spine stiffened as he stopped beside her and brushed the hair from her eyes with a feather-light touch, tucking the strands behind her ear. He removed her hair clip and tucked it into his pocket.

"Hey!"

"I hope our child has your silky hair. We're going to make a beautiful baby, Nicole."

She gulped at his rusty tone. Alarms screeched in her brain. She needed to get away from him. But her muscles ignored her frantic orders. A shiver worked down her spine and her nipples tightened. Her pulse and breathing quickened and her stomach fisted with desire. She wanted to order him to back off, but she couldn't find her voice.

His fingertips dragged down the sensitive side of her neck and rested on her collarbone. She reluctantly lifted her gaze to his and found his eyes focused on her mouth.

She wanted his kiss.

The realization shocked a gasp from her. How long had it been since she'd actually wanted to kiss someone? Not since Patrick. Sure, she'd dated in the past six years and endured dozens of mediocre good-night kisses, but she'd never craved one the way she did Ryan's. *Right now.* And that spelled disaster.

She tried to recall Patrick's face, to will his image to replace Ryan's in her mind's eye. She failed. Miserably.

One of Ryan's hands cupped her nape and gently massaged the knotted muscles. The other rested on her waist, pulling her forward. The simultaneous press of his lips and his body against hers sent shock waves of pleasure rippling through her. His mouth opened and closed, brushing hers, teasing and luring her into passion far out of her depths. He sucked her bottom lip between his, tugged gently with his teeth and then stroked her tender flesh inside with his tongue.

A current of desire crashed over her, washing

away her resistance and the reasons why this shouldn't happen. His hot, slick tongue caressed hers, and his palm gently covered her breast with a blanket of heat. A whirlpool of sensation twisted deep inside her.

Trying to dam her response was a waste of time. Her hands drifted to his hips, then a rising tide of hunger carried them to his shoulders. Her fingers tangled in his short, crisp, sun-warmed hair.

His hand scorched a trail from her nape to her bottom, kneading her, cupping her and pulling her closer. The ridge of his hardening flesh against her belly exhilarated her. She leaned into him, reveling in the novel sensations swamping her.

She couldn't take enough breath through her nose to keep the dizziness at bay. Her breast tingled beneath his thumb's caress, and she hungered for more. More of his kisses. More of his touch. More of his taste. As if he'd read her thoughts, he widened his stance, pulled her between his legs and plunged deeper into her mouth. He found her tight nipple and rolled it between his fingertips. A riptide of need tugged at her core, making her ache with an unfamiliar emptiness that yearned to be filled.

Why had she never wanted like this before? Why now? Why Ryan? Besides the life they'd inadvertently created, what power did he have over her?

Her fingers flexed involuntarily in a last-ditch effort to stop the insanity, and her nails scraped across the warm skin on his neck.

He shuddered and groaned into her mouth, rocking her like a rogue wave knocking a buoy off balance, and making her crave more of whatever it was he was doing to her body, her mind, her soul. But at the same time, her response startled her enough to make her realize this was the siren's song that lured her mother into so many meaningless affairs. Passion for a man you knew and cared little about.

Panic hit like a sobering plunge into Arctic waters. Nicole shoved against Ryan's chest, jerked free and, gulping in one desperate breath after another, backed as far away as the confines of the boat would allow.

She would not become her mother. No matter what Beth said.

Nicole had spent her adulthood proving she wasn't impetuous and that she always considered the consequences before taking action.

"Nicole." Ryan reached for her again, his eyes burning with hunger, but she evaded him. She *had* to evade him. The way he made her feel was too dangerous, too out of control.

"Ryan, we can't do this. This desire, this connection between us…it isn't real. We're both caught up in the magical moment of what we shared at the doctor's office today."

His eyes narrowed. "If you believe that, then you're fooling yourself."

Maybe so. "I can't become involved with a man who is trying to take my baby and destroy my relationship with my family."

"Our baby," he corrected again and this time a yawning emptiness opened deep inside her.

Their baby. The words resurrected a dream she'd abandoned long ago. A dream of having her own home and family with a man who adored her. A dream that had died when the man she loved married her sister.

"Stop saying that."

"Not saying it won't change the facts."

"I want to go ashore."

He caught her elbow. "I'd like to show you something first."

"I don't think—"

"My favorite spot in the river is about a mile from here. Our son or daughter will be seeing a lot of it."

He'd said the one thing guaranteed to keep her on board. "Boating isn't safe for a baby."

"I've told you before I don't take unnecessary risks. They make infant life jackets. I love the water, and I intend to share that interest with my child the way my grandfather shared his with me."

Instantly, an image of a gangly dark-haired, blue-eyed boy filled her mind. She did not need that cute picture in her head.

Gazes locked, tense silence stretched between them like an anchor rope. Did she dare go with Ryan? Eager to soak up anything she might possibly miss in her baby's future, she inclined her head. It would only take a few minutes, and she'd keep her distance from Ryan and his devastating kisses.

He released her arm and bent over, breaking the connection. When he straightened all traces of desire had vanished from his face. He held a ball cap and a life jacket which he'd pulled from one of the side compartments. He thrust the flotation device in her hands and gently settled the cap on her head.

"I don't have sunscreen on board. You'll need the hat. Keep the life jacket close by."

He pivoted abruptly, crossed to the wheel and fired the engine. The strength left Nicole's legs and she sank onto the bench seat clutching the life jacket to her chest.

After casting off the stern line, Ryan returned to the controls. Seconds later the boat glided smoothly away from the dock. Nicole released a slow breath. Kiss ended. Catastrophe averted.

But strangely, her relief felt a lot like disappointment, and the hunger gnawing at her stomach had nothing to do with delicious aromas emitting from the take-out bag on the bench beside her.

Eight

Mistake. The word reverberated in Ryan's head, drowning out the roar of the boat's inboard motor.

Kissing Nicole had been a mistake. Both times.

She was the marrying kind. He was not.

She was family oriented. He was not.

She put others first. He looked out for number one.

But damn, her lips, the feel of her breast filling his hand and her slender body against his had set him on fire. Not what he needed to be thinking when lunch was the only thing on the menu this afternoon, and common sense told him to aim for contract not consummation.

He pulled into his favorite cove, killed the engine and let momentum carry the boat toward the dock.

What better way to ensure custody of your kid than to marry the mother?

He immediately tossed the idea overboard like an anchor. He knew what a bad marriage could do to a child. Before she'd left his father, his mother had been demanding and needy and whined incessantly for more of her husband's attention. Ryan suspected he was enough like his workaholic father to guarantee he'd put his job first and his marriage last. He'd yet to find anything or anyone who interested him more than work. And he'd never found a woman he could trust.

An image of Nicole stretched out on his bed instead of the examination table infiltrated his brain. He shoved it aside, grabbed the bowline and looped the rope through the cleat, but the idea of hooking up with Nicole wouldn't let him go.

The boat rocked as she stood. "Aren't we trespassing?"

"With permission. This is one of the houses the

real estate agent is going to show us." He pointed to the For Sale sign hanging on the covered, screened enclosure on one end of the dock. He'd considered it a stroke of luck when he'd spotted the sign on his last cruise upriver.

"I thought you were going to show me your favorite spot."

"This cove is it. Not a lot of current. Good fishing. Room to wakeboard."

She looked wary and a little put out as she scanned the wide offshoot of the river. "Couldn't we have driven here?"

"That wouldn't have blown away your headache."

Her eyes narrowed. "I never said I had a headache."

"You didn't have to. I could see it in your face and in the stiff way you moved your head. That's why I took your hair clip. But the headache is gone now, isn't it?"

Her frown deepened. "Yes. But I thought you were going to change the appointment."

He shrugged. "Since we needed to cruise upriver to find a picnic spot anyway, there wasn't any reason to cancel. The house is vacant. We'll eat in the gazebo. The agent will meet us in thirty minutes to give us a quick tour."

He tied the stern line then grabbed Nicole's shoes and the food bag and set both onto the dock. After climbing from the boat he turned and offered her a hand. She hesitated before placing her palm in his. Even though he braced himself, the zap hit him harder and more intensely than before, probably because now he knew how good she felt against him.

"Put on your shoes. You don't want to risk a splinter." He shifted his grip to her sun-warmed biceps to help her balance. The heat of her skin made him think of hot bodies—hot *naked* bodies. Arousal percolated through him along with a strong urge to rest his hand over her belly and his baby that was almost too strong to resist.

As soon as she'd donned her sexy heels he released her and led the way into the large screened portion of the dock and set the bag on the picnic table. It was much safer to focus on food rather than the forbidden.

"This is nice," she offered with her head tipped

back to view the ceiling fan hanging from the steeply pitched tongue-and-groove ceiling. The honey-colored varnished wood had aged beautifully, but the perfectly mitered joints weren't what caught his attention. His gaze traced the line of Nicole's throat to the pulse fluttering beneath her pale skin.

The pose was purely sexual with her back and neck arched and her lips parted. She looked like a woman reaching climax. And the most surprising thing was that he'd swear her posture wasn't deliberate. He was used to women trolling their sensuality like bait, but he'd bet his bike Nicole had no idea she'd just sent him into testosterone overload.

He shook his head and resumed unpacking. Seeing a little of her skin had obviously short-circuited his brain.

She turned her attention to the two-story house sitting on the crest of a hill with the lush lawn terraced into two large, flat areas. "This property has the kind of fencing along the waterfront and the dock that I mentioned. It would be safe for a child to play in this yard."

"Fencing will keep a timid kid out of trouble, but a curious one will find a way around it."

"Is that the voice of experience speaking?" The look she cut him from under her lashes blasted him with a shot of heat below his belt. Did she have any idea how strong a punch the combination of her light eyes, sparkling with amusement, and long dark lashes packed? Probably not.

"I was an inquisitive kid. Were you?"

She bit her bottom lip and averted her face. "I found my share of scrapes to get into. Beth always helped me out of them by running interference with my parents."

That piqued his interested. "What kind of things?"

She fussed with the lid of the chicken box and shrugged. "Just dumb stuff to get my parents' attention. Nothing illegal."

"I wouldn't have pegged you as the mischievous type. Trying to get our parents' attention is something we have in common."

She stared at him for a moment then swallowed. "How old were you when your parents separated?"

"Ten. Old enough to understand most of what was going on and resent the hell out of it."

"If your parents were miserable together, it's better that they separated."

"Better than me being the bone between two fighting dogs?" Damn, he hadn't meant to say that. He wasn't a whiner. The past was over.

"Better than being forgotten." She ducked her head again as if she regretted her words.

Ryan had researched Nicole's family since the Labor Day picnic enough to know hers wasn't average. Her parents' exploits often made front page in the society section.

"You're not forgettable, Nicole."

Where had that come from? Put a lid on it, Patrick.

She stared up at him with rounded eyes. The urge to kiss her pushed him forward. Her cheeks flushed. She turned abruptly and looked at the house. "The style is reminiscent of the New Orleans French Quarter. I love the wrought iron railings and arches."

He wanted to know her story, but knowing meant caring and that wasn't part of his plan. But damned if he could stop the questions pounding his brain or the anger stirring through him. "Did your parents neglect you?"

"Neglect? No. But my mother was a firm believer in tough love and living with the consequences of your actions. I guess I wanted her to be the milk-and-cookies and kiss-your-boo-boos type." She sighed and shook her head. "Tell me about the house."

He let her change the subject because thinking of a kid needing a hug reminded him of the days he'd sat on the front steps waiting in vain for his father to come home. "The house has four thousand square feet, five bedrooms and six baths. There's a nanny apartment over the garages."

"A nanny apartment?"

"Yes."

"You're going to hire a nanny?"

"It won't be any different if the child is in day care except for the on-site convenience factor."

"HAMC's day care is just down the hall. I can log in and watch the baby from my desk, and I can spend my lunch hour with him or her."

"When I work at home I'll be under the same

roof." That hadn't been part of his original plan, but it sounded feasible—if the house were laid out right and had a decent home office setup. A hands-on dad like his had been before his mother turned the house into a battlefield every time his father came to visit. Eventually his dad had quit coming.

He yanked himself back to the present. "I'm familiar with the builder. He does quality work. The neighborhood has a pool, tennis courts and a gym in the clubhouse."

If his father didn't consider this a stable, put-down-roots address, then nothing would please him.

Nicole nodded. "Not having a pool on the property is a plus."

He finished unpacking the plastic utensils and paper plates. The delicious aromas filled his nose and his stomach growled in anticipation. He gestured to their picnic. "Help yourself."

She wasted no time filling her plate, and after he'd done the same she scooped up a spoonful of her peach cobbler and popped it between her lips.

Dessert first. His kind of girl.

None of that. No woman was his kind of girl—

except the temporary ones who provided sex or an escort when a formal affair required one.

He turned his attention to an appetite he could safely satisfy. The fried chicken was crispy on the outside and juicy on the inside—just the way he liked it. Not as good as his grandmother's recipe, but close.

Nicole paused between bites, her aqua eyes finding his. "If you had an unhappy childhood, what makes you think you'll know how to be a good parent?"

He chewed and swallowed while he decided how much to share. "I never said I was unhappy. Like fifty-some percent of all marriages my parents' ended in divorce. I still had good role models in my maternal grandparents and my father when he made an appearance."

His mother had often dumped him on his grandparents when his father wasn't around, but those days with his grandparents had been some of the best of his life. Since he needed Nicole to feel secure in the child's future, he decided to volunteer some information.

"My grandfather shared his love of the water

with me. My grandmother was a firm believer in the idle-hands-find-trouble theory. She taught me to cook and clean up after myself." The softening expression in Nicole's eyes set off alarm bells. "Your folks stayed together, how is that going to make you a better parent?"

Her chin tilted at a defensive angle. "We're not talking about me. Beth will be a great mom. And Patrick will be an amazing father. He's kind and patient and never raises his voice. And he's talented. He can play almost any musical instrument. He teaches music at the University of Tennessee. His family is warm, welcoming, generous and tight-knit. They have family reunions every summer and get together each Christmas. His parents are amazing. This child will be very lucky to have them as grandparents."

The flush on her cheeks when she talked about the greedy little weasel annoyed him because, without a doubt, Patrick Ryan would have taken the payout Ryan had offered if his wife hadn't intervened. He might still be convinced to take it.

"Sounds like you should have married him instead of your sister."

Nicole froze then paled. She focused on eating her cobbler.

He didn't like the vibe coming his way—especially when added to the fact that her brother-in-law had been the intended father of her child.

"Is there something going on between you and Patrick Ryan?"

She gulped down a mouthful and carefully wiped her lips with a paper napkin. "What a ridiculous question. Of course not."

"He's ten or fifteen years older than you and your degree is from UT. Did you fall for your professor, Nicole?"

She hid her face by sipping from her cup of sweet iced tea, but her red cheeks gave him his answer. For some reason the idea of her with Professor Ryan made him want to hit something.

She finally lowered the cup. "My private life is none of your business unless it pertains to the health of this baby."

Ryan leaned back against the railing, studying her and wondering how the professor could be dumb enough to have chosen the wrong sister. Anyone that stupid had no business fathering or parenting a child. “How did he end up with your sister?”

She pushed the thick vegetable stew around on her sectioned plate with her fork. “Tell me more about the house.”

His lips twitched at her obvious evasion. “Were you in one of his classes?”

“That’s none of your business.”

“It is if he makes a habit of hooking up with his students.”

She looked insulted. “Patrick has never cheated on Beth.”

She seemed determined to defend the little twerp. “Are you sure of that?”

“From the moment he laid eyes on her he never wanted anyone else.” She looked down. Her fingers clenched her fork. “We need to finish eating if we’re going to tour the house and get me back to work.”

“Answer my questions first.”

She abandoned her utensils. “Why is it relevant?”

“I’m trying to understand why you would relinquish this baby when it is tearing you apart.”

"Because it's the right thing to do," she almost shouted, the pain clear in her voice.

"Most women will fight to keep their kids even if they don't want them just for the power it gives them over their ex." Realization hit him like a falling concrete wall. "That's it. This baby is the linchpin. It's your connection to your brother-in-law even after he divorces your sister."

"No!"

An uglier thought occurred to him. "Or maybe he's leaving your sister for you. She's a real ball breaker, and you were supposed to be having his kid. Maybe he was going to boot your sister out of that house in the suburbs, and you're planning to take her place."

Every speck of color fled her face. "How dare you. And you're wrong. Even if Beth and Patrick did separate I would never take him back." Her eyes widened and her lips slammed shut as she regretted the slip.

Being right didn't fill him with satisfaction. "So he was yours first. Did Beth steal him?"

"Stop it."

"What happened, Nicole? You brought him

home to meet the family and big sister stole him?" He could tell from her shattered expression that he'd guessed correctly, and while he regretted acting like a prick by ripping the scab off an old wound, his rage toward the weasel who'd hurt her far surpassed courtesy.

She stood, hands fisted by her side. "Take me back. Now."

"Does the truth make you uncomfortable?"

"If you won't take me, I'll hitch a ride with your real estate agent."

"Patrick Ryan is an idiot. You're better off without him."

She stalked out of the screened porch and up the dock toward the house. Ryan watched her go. What in the hell had gotten into him? He'd never been the type to torment a woman like that. But Nicole's feelings for the jackass had irritated his stomach like the burn of cheap tequila.

Best to give her time to cool off and him time to get his head back on straight because losing control with her wasn't going to get him anywhere but in trouble.

One thing was certain, he decided as he

repacked the remnants of their lunch, Nicole's bastard of a brother-in-law was not getting his hands on this baby. Ryan intended to make damned sure of it—no matter how far he had to go to guarantee success.

Nicole could practically hear the sound of children's laughter echoing through the empty house, and her heart ached. She would never have a home like this or the family the bright, spacious rooms called out for. She wouldn't let herself.

She couldn't marry when her heart still belonged to Patrick. She'd seen how tying yourself to the wrong person turned out. If her mother had married the man she loved instead of the one her father had chosen for her as part of a business deal, then the Hightower family would have been filled with love instead of headed by two people miserably and grudgingly doing their duty. Two people who should have divorced long ago if the hateful words they'd shouted at each other were the truth.

Nicole visually tracked Ryan's progress across the lush green lawn from her position in the open set of double French doors leading from the huge eat-in kitchen to the brick patio that overlooked the river and boat dock.

He approached the tree house built in one corner of the backyard. Looking up, he circled the base suspended a yard above his head. Next he examined the ladder, shook it and then tested the bottom tread with his foot.

The real estate agent chuckled beside Nicole as Ryan climbed and disappeared through the wooden floor above him. "Boys will be boys."

"I guess so." But her brothers had never had a tree house. Planes, boats, vacation homes, yes. Nicole had taken advantage of the last two, but not the first. She'd always been interested in learning to fly, but Beth had cautioned her that unless she wanted to be an absentee mother like theirs she'd better leave piloting to the men.

And now, the irony was she wouldn't be a mother at all.

The shutters of the simple wooden structure opened and Ryan's face appeared. "Come on up, Nicole."

Surprised, she startled. "I don't think so."

"It's structurally sound. Don't tell me you're chicken."

Chicken? Her spine snapped straight. He had no idea how often she'd heard that dare. Or how many times it had gotten her in trouble. As the youngest, she'd had a lot to prove.

"You know you want to see the kind of place your child will be playing in," he added.

Dirty. He'd hit her in her most vulnerable spot. She approached the structure, her heels sinking into the grass with each step. At the bottom of the ladder she kicked off her shoes and climbed. Her head cleared the opening, and she gasped in delight at the miniature home. Small scaled wooden tables, chairs and even a bunk bed filled the space.

Ryan cupped her elbow and helped her stand. Even after he released her the heat of his touch lingered on her skin. Despite the vaulted ceiling complete with skylights, Ryan dwarfed the space. She turned a slow circle. "Any child would love this hideout."

"My father and I designed a clubhouse very similar to this."

Something in the tone of his voice caught her

attention. She leaned back to study his face. "Did you build it?"

The regret in his eyes gave her the answer before he shook his head. "My parents divorced before we could start."

Her heart ached for the confused child he must have been. She wanted her baby to have a father who would plan tree houses and fishing trips. A father like Ryan. Patrick would never be the type to risk looking silly by acting boyish. She couldn't picture him stooping in a kid's playhouse or scaling a homemade ladder.

Her fingers curled around Ryan's forearm in an offer of support before she realized what she was doing.

He pressed his hand overtop hers before she could pull away and his gaze drilled hers. "I was out of line earlier when I harassed you about your brother-in-law. I apologize."

Surprised, she stared at him. His words demonstrated yet another difference between the two men. Ryan regretted hurting her feelings. Patrick had never apologized for devastating her life. "Apology accepted."

Her anger toward Ryan had already dissipated, anyway. She couldn't blame him for putting the puzzle pieces of her life together, and accurately, too. It wasn't his fault that she didn't like the segment he'd chosen to highlight.

"It's his loss, Nicole." He released her hand but her reprieve was short-lived. One long finger brushed her cheek, sending a frisson of awareness over her.

She couldn't risk another one of his devastating kisses. She backed to the open window, turned and looked out over the yard, house and river below. "This house couldn't be more perfect if you'd drawn the plans yourself."

He joined her, his elbows and upper arms bumping hers as he leaned on the narrow sill beside her. "It's not bad."

"*Not bad?* Ryan, every safety feature that could be added has been. The home office is amazing, and this yard and tree house are wonderful. The kitchen is made for big family dinners. Everything about this property cries out for children."

Ryan scanned the property and then his eyes met hers. "Don't do it."

Confused, she frowned. “Don’t do what?”

“Relinquish.”

She gasped at the intrusion of real life. “We’ve been over this, Ryan.”

“You claim Beth and Patrick want this baby, but if that were true nothing would have kept them from that appointment today. Nothing could have kept me from being there.”

Nicole winced at the accuracy of his statement. In weak moments, she’d thought the same thing. She straightened and crossed the tiny space. “They were busy.”

The excuse was pathetic and, she suspected, untrue.

“The kid is not theirs. They’ve done nothing to help you with expenses. Break the contract, Nicole. You have two valid reasons for doing so.”

“But I—”

“Don’t drag this kid through the hell you know is coming. I’ve seen enough of my friends’ marriages end to recognize when there’s no love left, and it’s time to cut your losses. I’m sure you have, too. Beth and Patrick have reached that point. You can see it in their distance when they’re together.”

His words chiseled away another chunk of her confidence that giving up her baby was the right thing to do. A cold knot formed in her middle. "A baby will make them happy."

"Are you absolutely certain of that? A baby is more likely to increase their problems than erase them."

She couldn't respond. Not the way she wanted to.

"My lawyer claims breaking the contract will be almost impossible given the legal precedents already set, and changing my mind could tear my family apart."

"Or it could set your sister free from an obligation she no longer wants to keep." The certainty in his voice and in his cobalt eyes ignited a spark of hope in her heart, but she was afraid to fan the flame only to have it snuffed out.

He'd voiced her greatest fear and her greatest hope—something she hadn't even allowed herself to put into words. Was he right? Did Beth want out of their agreement now that they knew the baby wasn't Patrick's? Was that why she kept delaying the announcement? Nicole couldn't blame her sister if she'd changed her mind. Maybe Beth was sticking by her promise out of a sense of duty.

Nicole wanted to keep her baby with every fiber of her being, ached for it to have two parents who would love it, cherish it and want the best for it. For a moment in this perfect little cabin in the trees she believed she and Patrick could be those parents. Maybe not in the traditional, married sense, but parents who shared custody and love of the child they'd created.

But she'd given her word, and she would not break it unless Beth and Patrick wanted out of their agreement. Otherwise, she could lose everything. Her job. Her family. And her baby.

And then she'd have nothing and no one.

Nine

Over. Finally.

Nicole closed her file and exhaled in relief Friday afternoon as the Patrick Architectural team of Ryan and his father exited her office.

She'd barely been able to concentrate during her first consult with them. Simple facts had been hard to retrieve. Not that anyone who didn't know her well would have noticed, but it had been a constant struggle to stick to her planned pitch because every time Ryan had made eye contact, her thoughts had scattered like fall leaves. And her mind would wander off to replay the kisses she'd shared with him and the carrot of custody he'd dangled in front of her two days ago. Two days in which Beth had avoided Nicole's calls and hadn't come into the office.

"I'll see you tonight."

Ryan's voice brought her head up. He'd stopped in her doorway instead of following his father out. "I'm sorry?"

"At the party."

"Party? What par—" Surprise made her breath catch. With all the upheaval in her life she'd completely forgotten the annual black-tie affair for Hightower Air's employees and clients was tonight. "Of course. It slipped my mind."

One dark eyebrow lifted. "Have a date?"

Trick question? Ah, but Ryan wouldn't know. "I never take a date to company affairs."

"Why?"

"Because I talk shop and it bores most men to sleep."

"It won't bore me. I'll pick you up."

Exactly what she didn't need. "Thank you, but I have to be there early to make sure everything is ready."

"Beth and Patrick should see us as a united team."

The battle resumed inside her, but she knew herself well enough to know that if Beth and Patrick truly wanted this child, then she would not deny them their hearts' desire even though it would break hers. She shifted in her pumps, afraid to commit, but very aware of what she'd lose if she did…and if she didn't.

"I haven't decided to take that route yet. I need to talk to them first."

"No point in both of us going stag. I don't mind arriving early."

He moved into her personal space, crowding her against the leather sofa where they'd concluded their meeting. Her calves pressed the cool upholstery. His heat, his tangy scent and his sheer physical presence overwhelmed her. Her brain screamed a warning. She couldn't remember ever being this aware of any other person in her life. He felt it, too. She could see the awareness in his parted lips and expanding pupils. Her pulse skipped. She swallowed the flood of moisture in her mouth.

"I have to be there at eight." She wanted to slap her hand over the errant orifice. Where had that come from? What had happened to the polite refusal she'd intended? She hadn't meant to imply an invitation with her tone.

"I'll pick you up at twenty before." Ryan held her gaze without touching her, but he might as well. Every cell in her being tap-danced with excitement.

She wished he would leave.

She wished he would kiss her.

She wished she knew what she wanted. Being wishy-washy ticked her off, and everything about their complicated situation confused her.

"Good job today. You impressed the hell out of my father when you took him through the plane and covered all the technical jargon. Brains and beauty are one hell of a potent combo. You and HAMC have certainly exceeded our expectations to this point."

His praise took her aback and warmed her cheeks. She decided to focus on the business component of his comment rather than the personal reaction she couldn't understand. "Thank you, Ryan. I hope we continue to do so."

It was her job to orient her clients to their new aircraft, to walk them through the aircraft they'd chosen and to explain the services HAMC could provide—and of course to offer more services which could be had for an additional fee. Few ever bothered to express gratitude for her hard work. Meeting their requirements was her job, one they took for granted she'd do successfully. She only heard about it when she failed to meet their expectations which, thank goodness, was a rarity.

Which brought her back to that strangely intimate moment in the tree house. For a moment there she'd felt closer to him than to anyone ever in her life. He knew her darkest secret and didn't despise her for it.

Ryan reached into his coat pocket and pulled out a small wrapped package the size of a paperback book. "For you."

A gift? She took it with reservations and tore the glossy yellow paper. A white picture frame hand-painted with pastel-colored baby blocks held the ultrasound photograph the doctor had snapped at the moment when their baby's little fingers had wiggled almost as if he or she had been waving hello. Emotion welled inside her. Nicole pressed her fingers to her lips to stop the sob pushing its way up her throat.

"That's our son. Or daughter." His voice had a rough quality as if he were as emotionally affected as she was.

She inhaled a ragged breath. Her eyes and throat burned as she traced the shadowy outline. She suspected he'd be the kind of father who offered praise and encouragement along with his time and guidance. The kind she'd always wanted. The kind every child deserved.

"Thank you, Ryan."

"You're welcome." She jerked at the contact of his fingertip on her cheek and then he dragged a hot sweep of temptation that stopped at the corner of her mouth. Her lips parted. She tasted salt and realized he'd mapped a tear she hadn't noticed escaping.

"I'll see you tonight." He turned abruptly and strode out of her office, leaving her with a hurricane of emotion twisting through her system and an ache for…something she couldn't name.

She clutched the frame to her chest. He couldn't have given her anything more meaningful. And she didn't miss the symbolism. He wanted to give her their baby.

"Tell me you bought a killer new dress for this thing." Lea's quip jerked her out of her trance.

Nicole wasn't ready to share Ryan's paternity yet because that would lead to twenty questions—questions she didn't have the answers to yet. She turned toward her desk, surreptitiously wiping her cheeks, and slipped the photo into a drawer.

"Nicole, are you okay?"

"Yes. But I'm embarrassed to confess that with the pregnancy and all, I forgot about the gala."

"Well, now you have a hot date with a steamy guy who happens to be loaded and doesn't mind that you're pregnant with another man's baby. We have work to do, girlfriend."

She winced at Lea's misconception, but didn't have the fortitude to explain the situation at the moment.

She mentally searched her closet and discarded

her entire wardrobe. What was wrong with her? Anything she had would have been suitable. Ten minutes ago.

But not anymore.

"I guess you're right. I don't have anything to wear."

Lea threw an arm around her shoulders. "We have no time to shop. We'll swing by my place. It's on your way home. Lucky for you I'm an outlet sales addict, and I buy more than I need. I have a ruby-red Calvin Klein halter dress that will look great on you."

Lea, an admitted shopaholic, had gushed about the dress for a week after she'd found it on the clearance rack. "I can't take that. You haven't worn it yet."

"Trust me, the pleated sweetheart neckline will look better on you with your…accentuated assets than it does on my flat chest. Ryan can't help but notice those babies." Lea's nod indicated Nicole's pregnancy-swollen breasts, and Nicole groaned.

"Lea, stop matchmaking."

"Who's matchmaking? I'm just stating the

obvious. I need a cold shower after seeing that little exchange between you two. You're going to look hot, and he's going to notice."

That was not what Nicole needed since resisting temptation in the form of Ryan Patrick was at the top of her list.

Nicole surreptitiously glanced at her Cartier watch. Her evening had been a total failure thus far. Not by anyone else's standards, but by hers.

Her goal tonight while having her entire family in the same room was to remind herself of what she'd lose if she chose to be selfish.

Instead, as she stood on the balcony overlooking the elegant ballroom below and scanned the guests, seeking out her siblings scattered far and wide across the travertine floor, she realized how alone each of them was in the crowd.

Trent, the oldest and company CEO, stood with his babe de jour and the president of HAMC's largest client. Trent's twin, Brent, with his usual Scotch in hand, was nowhere near his pregnant wife. No surprise there.

Beth and Patrick were side by side, but at the same time miles apart. When, why and how had that happened? Had the stress of infertility caused their emotional separation or was it something more? Would the baby fix the situation or make it worse? Nicole needed to look Beth in the eye and ask if she wanted out of their agreement, but her sister had been avoiding her.

You would have thought having to rely on each other while growing up would have brought the Hightower siblings closer and made them friends as well as family. It hadn't. Other than the same parents and the same employer, they had nothing in common.

Nicole wanted a tight familial connection for her child. On her first date with Patrick he'd taken her to his family reunion. She'd seen what families should be like and craved it ever since.

Her mother sidled up to the banister beside her. Her gaze ran over Nicole. "You look quite lovely tonight. Not your usual style, but the gown works for you."

"Thank you, Mother."

A heavy silence descended between them.

Nicole resumed her search for Ryan's dark hair, broad shoulders and black tux.

"Nicole, if you have a problem you can come to me."

Nicole blinked and looked at her mother in surprise, but Jacqueline sipped her champagne and focused on the guests gathered below.

The shoulder her mother offered came a little too late. They'd never had the kind of relationship where Nicole could comfortably pour out her fears—especially something of this magnitude. "I'll keep that in mind."

Jacqueline turned then and lifted a hand as if to touch Nicole's face, but dropped it without making contact. "I haven't always been there for you. I'm just now beginning to realize and regret how much I've missed." Her heavily made-up eyes echoed the sentiment of her words. "Enjoy your evening and your beau."

Her mother stalked away leaving a cloud of Armani Diamonds perfume behind.

Did her mother's regrets have something to do with the daughter she'd given up? Nicole found Lauren, the newest addition to the family. Lauren was living proof that everyone needed to be connected somehow. After her father's death she had come looking for her relatives. Unfortunately for her, that family happened to be the aloof Hightowers instead of a warm, welcoming clan like Patrick's.

Not your problem. You have more than enough on your plate.

Where was Ryan? Nicole didn't see him anywhere in the ballroom. Her heart missed a beat. Had he grown tired of her working the crowd and her clients and left? He hadn't seemed to mind her preoccupation. In fact, having him by her side while she greeted the guests tonight had felt good, and for the first time she'd felt like part of a couple. Listening to him interact with them had taught her a valuable lesson. Ryan was smart and ambitious and had a memory like a steel trap. She'd have to be careful not to underestimate him.

"You haven't danced with me."

She jumped at his voice behind her and spun around. "I haven't danced with anyone. I've been working. Parties like this are an opportunity for me to have face time with clients I only talk to via phone or e-mail the rest of the year."

"And you excel at making each client feel valued. That's an important trait in my business, as well."

More praise. It warmed her all over.

His brilliant blue gaze slid from her face to her breasts which tightened under his perusal, then on to her waist and back up again. She was used to dressing to please herself, but the instant she'd seen the approval in his eyes when he'd arrived at her home earlier, she'd been glad she'd let Lea talk her into this sexier little number.

He offered his hand, palm up. "The band is about to begin the final song of the night. Dance with me."

The excited leap of her pulse sent a warning. One she decided to ignore. What could one dance hurt? They were in a roomful of people. Nothing could happen.

She placed her hand in his and let him lead her to the grand staircase. Heads turned as they descended to the main ballroom. She did her best to ignore the curious eyes, but she couldn't deny feeling a little like Cinderella, the belle of the ball with the handsome prince at her side.

Ryan in a tux took her breath away. The epitome of tall, dark and handsome, his shoulders filled out his black jacket and his bow tie framed his square jaw. He was easily the most attractive man present tonight, but his appeal was more than just good looks. His allure derived from the confident way he carried himself, the intelligence shining from his gorgeous blue eyes and in the way he made her feel like the most desirable woman present. And wasn't that a fairy tale? She shot him a sideway smile which he returned with knee-weakening potency.

He led her into the middle of the dance floor and pulled her into his arms. The gentle impact of his big, solid body against hers knocked the breath right out of her—not from the force of the contact, but from the sheer strength of the combustion between them.

She inhaled deeply and his tangy scent filled her lungs. One wide palm splayed across her back. His hard thigh slotted between hers, and with each step his hips brushed her tummy over the tiny life they'd created. The ruby sateen fabric of her dress did nothing to block the pooling heat his proximity created. Ryan overwhelmed and overpowered her senses, and for once she let herself be swept away instead of fighting the current of desire.

Her eyes locked with his, and as he guided her around the floor awareness of the curious gazes of her family and coworkers faded until her focus narrowed to just him and her and the bond they shared.

The sad fact of the matter was that she felt more connected to Ryan Patrick, a man she hadn't known existed three weeks ago, than she did to any of her family members. He'd understood how much the ultrasound peek at their child had meant to her, and it had apparently meant as much to him. Her own sister hadn't cared enough to show up to meet the child she planned to adopt and had promised to love.

Ryan had noticed when she had a headache and insisted on an impromptu picnic to help her destress. He read her in a way she couldn't remember anyone else ever doing. Patrick certainly hadn't.

Ryan was in fact the only person in her life who understood the pain of losing her child.

The press of his leg against her center sent a rush of arousal through her, making her entire body come alive with awareness. Her breaths rasped audibly, and her pulse roared in her ears drowning out the music of the band behind her. Need radiated from her center.

She wanted Ryan in a way she'd never wanted anyone before. Just for tonight she needed to feel connected to someone who understood the tangle of emotions tearing her apart, someone who wanted to give instead of take. She'd handle the consequences, be what they may, tomorrow.

As if she'd telegraphed her thoughts, Ryan's pupils expanded. He leaned forward and his lips grazed her ear with spine-tingling results. "Let's get out of here."

His gruff whisper caused the hairs on her nape to lift. "Yes. Please."

Keeping possession of her hand, he strode toward the exit at a brisk pace. He didn't look left or right or pause to speak to anyone. The limo slid to a stop in front of them even before they'd reached the curb as if the driver had been waiting for them to appear. Ryan hustled her into the backseat.

"My place," he told the driver through the open window between the front and back compartments before pushing the button to slide the tinted glass closed.

Nicole knew she should argue, knew exactly where they were headed if she didn't. Not just to Ryan's condo, but to his bed. She subdued her protests even though crossing the intimacy line was something she rarely allowed herself to do.

Ryan's arm slid around her waist. He scooped her into his lap in the darkened car and slanted his mouth across hers, capturing her gasp on his tongue. His fingers tangled in her hair, cupping her nape and holding her captive while one hungry kiss melded into another. He kissed like he did everything else: with deliberation, precision and devastating skill. The two kisses they'd shared previously had been tame compared to the way he consumed her mouth tonight.

He stroked, sucked, nipped her mouth with urgent passion that incited and invited her own.

His other hand caressed her back, her lower belly and then slid toward her breast.

Her body stilled in anticipation as a response she couldn't ignore swelled within her. She wanted his touch, ached for it. Arching her back, she pressed her breast into his palm.

Her stomach fluttered like the tail of a kite in a strong wind, and a line of tension formed between her nipples and her core. Each brush of his thumb against her stretched it tighter. The burn deep inside made her shift her hips. His groan rumbled down her throat. He arched against her, pressing a thick erection to her bottom.

And then he yanked his mouth free and hissed in a breath. "If you'd rather go home alone, tell me now."

She couldn't see his eyes in the shadowy interior, but his gravelly tone and his hard body said he wanted her as much as she wanted him.

Run, the way you always do.

But she didn't want to run this time, didn't want to play it safe. She wanted to surrender instead of holding back, wanted to revel in wanting someone as much as he wanted her. It was only physical. She knew that. But she and Ryan shared so many things. A past rebellious spirit. An interest in the child she carried. And now a passion that couldn't be denied.

Being in his arms felt right. Scarily, eerily right. She couldn't believe making love with him would be a mistake. For her sake, for her baby's sake, she had to see where this would lead.

"I want to go home with you, Ryan."

Nicole wasn't the first woman Ryan had brought to his place, and she wouldn't be the last.

But this time felt different.

In the past the need for raw sex had been his primary agenda. Satisfy the hunger. Take the lady home. End of story.

With Nicole, he wanted to go slow, to linger over her subtle curves despite the urgency burning his gut. He wanted to map each inch of the body nurturing his child.

Even more, he wanted to crawl inside her head and understand why she was willing to make such a great personal sacrifice for someone she loved. Such selflessness was beyond his experience. In his world people always looked out for their own interests. Was Nicole truly that generous? Or was she using this baby to sink a hook in her brother-in-law? He wanted to believe the latter, but everything he'd learned about her pointed to the former.

Lacing his fingers through hers, he led her toward his bedroom without turning on the lights. Moonbeams from the uncurtained windows painted a glistening white path on the polished dark slate floors. His platform bed rested half in shadow, half in moonlight. He urged Nicole toward the light. He wanted to see every inch of her.

The rug surrounding his bed silenced the tap of her heels. He turned and soaked up the view. She'd left her hair down tonight. Curled strands draped over her shoulders, the ends teasing the top of her dress. The shiny red fabric hugged and lifted her breasts, tempting him, making his mouth water for a taste and his hands twitch for a touch. Her perfume, a light, floral scent, teased him. The whisper of her rapid breathing echoed his own.

"Your doctor said this was safe?" he confirmed.

"Yes. You heard her."

The fiery blush that had covered Nicole's face following the doctor's unsolicited statement returned. Twenty-eight and she still blushed. Interesting.

He cupped her warm cheek, stroked her silky soft skin. His fingers drifted down over the pulse fluttering at the base of her neck. That wild beat, combined with her parted lips and darkened eyes telegraphed her desire. His body received the signal loud and clear and multiplied it exponentially.

"You look beautiful tonight." He hadn't told her earlier because she'd been skittish. Who was he kidding? She'd taken his breath when she opened her door. He'd barely been able to think straight let alone form coherent sentences.

Her throat worked beneath his thumb as she swallowed. "Thank you."

He traced her collarbone then the narrow strap of her dress to the red material curving over the swells of her breasts. She gasped when he dipped his fingers into her warm shadowy cleavage, and then her chest shuddered on a ragged exhalation.

Nicole Hightower in full war paint was a sight to behold, and watching her work tonight had been impressive. She'd been poised and confident and had her clients eating out of her hand. The combination was sexy as hell.

He felt a twinge of guilt for using the attraction between them against her, but shoved it aside and kissed her again, savoring the taste of her soft lips and the warmth of her body pressed against his. He outlined her waist, her hips, and then followed her spine upward to locate her zipper tab between her shoulder blades. His knuckles brushed warm skin, smoother than the satin of her dress, as he tugged the zipper down. He eased the garment from her shoulders.

She wasn't wearing a bra. Her breasts weren't large, but what she had was perfectly shaped. Round and full, the nipples hard and dusky-pink. No tan lines. He swallowed the rush of saliva filling his mouth, and pushed the fabric over her hips, leaving her in lacy red panties and her heels. He looked her up and down. Exquisite. How had he ever mistaken her subtle curves for skinny?

She braced a hand on his shoulder as she

stepped free of her gown. Wanting her hands on his skin, he resented the barrier of clothing between them. As soon as she regained her balance, he shrugged out of his tux coat, tossed it toward the bench at the end of his bed and tackled his bow tie.

He hungrily drank her in with his eyes as he worked the buttons of his shirt free. She watched him, shifting on her feet and dampening her lips with her tongue. The fire building within him blazed hotter. Her skin was as pale as cream in the moonlight, her fingers fiddling nervously by her sides. He wanted those restless fingers on him. He shucked his shirt and kicked off his shoes.

"You're beautiful. Perfect." He reached for his belt, but the leather resisted him before giving way.

She covered her breasts. "I'm not usually so…pregnancy has made them larger."

He reached out and brushed her hands away, grazing her nipples in the process. Her gasp rent the air, mingling with the whistle of his indrawn breath as he dragged his knuckles over her stiff peaks again just for the pleasure of feeling the soft little beads bump over his skin.

He cupped her, thumbed the tips then bent to capture one with his lips because he couldn't wait another second to taste her. Her back arched, offering him more which he greedily took, sucking her deep into his mouth. He rolled his tongue around the tip and gently grazed her with his teeth.

She shivered in his arms and speared her fingers through his hair, holding him close as he sampled one soft mound and then the other. Grasping her waist, he backed toward the leather bench at the foot of his bed and sat. He pulled Nicole between his legs and feasted on her breasts.

Her nails dug into his scalp, and her soft moan filled the room. Fighting the urgency telling him to hurry, he smoothed a hand from her breast to her belly, reverently stroking the barely discernable sign that his child rested beneath.

His son or daughter.

His and Nicole's.

No. His. He couldn't settle for less than full custody.

His lips followed the trail his hand had blazed. He sipped and laved her skin, letting her unique flavor coat his tongue and her fragrance fill his nostrils. The scent of her arousal combined with her perfume, and his groin engorged in appreciation.

He caressed her long legs, his fingertips tracing the smooth skin covering her lean muscles, until he reached her ankles and the tiny buckles on her sandals. It took one hundred percent of his concentration to find the coordination to make his fingers work the narrow straps and remove her shoes. When he finished he hooked his thumbs in the lacy band of her panties and tugged them down her legs.

Dark curls surrounded her center, some of the tendrils already glistening with arousal. As soon as he'd discarded her lingerie he traced the damp line, finding her slick swollen flesh. She jerked and her breath hitched. He wanted more. Wanted to hear the sound she made when she came, feel her shudder and clench around him. Need drew his body up tight and hard. His pulse roared in his ears.

Recapturing a stiff dusky tip with his mouth, he matched the suckling and stroking of his tongue to the tempo of his fingers. Nicole's nails dug into his shoulders. He nudged her knees apart, widening her stance so he could pleasure her better. Within moments her legs began to quiver and her breath to quicken. Her back bowed and then, muscles tensing, she jerked as a whimper spilled from her mouth. He rose quickly to capture the remnants of her cry with his lips.

As her spasms died down, she clung to him, hung on him, her weight a delicious burden, her heat like a crackling fire. He broke the kiss and stared into her flushed face and slumberous eyes. He'd never seen a more alluring sight.

He had to have her. Now.

Grasping her hand, he backed toward the head of the bed, ripped the spread off with a yank that sent pillows flying and urged her onto the sheets.

She inched backward onto the mattress, her legs parting intermittently and giving him flashes of her damp center as she moved to the middle. That he believed the peep show unintentional made it all that more exciting. But that was Nicole. She had no idea how sensual she was.

And he had no business taking advantage of her. But the ends justified the means, and at least his desire for her was honest and intense and unlike anything he'd ever experienced before.

He shed the rest of his clothes in record time and eased over her. Bracing himself on straight arms, he slowly lowered his weight onto her until he had full body contact from ankles to lips. He didn't want to hurt her, but her skin branded him and her mouth devoured his. His erection rested against her smooth, hot stomach, and he had to grit his teeth to keep from driving against her. She felt so damned good.

He eased one knee between hers and then the other, opening her to him. It took everything he had not to ram hard and fast into her wetness. Remembering the life she cradled, he took himself in hand and stroked his rock hard flesh against her, teasing her swollen center and coating himself with her moisture to ease entry. He waited until she tensed and a flush covered her cheeks, and then he eased inside one gut-wrenching inch at a time, sliding deep into her body until he couldn't go any farther.

Her slick heat surrounded him and hunger ravaged him. He used his thumb to caress her, circling until she went over the edge. The rhythmic clenching of her internal muscles set him ablaze. A groan burst from his throat. He bore down on every cell in his being to keep from losing control. When he had a grip on his raging desire he dared to meet her aqua gaze. "You okay?"

"Yes," she all but hissed through kiss-swollen lips. "It feels good. *You* feel good, Ryan."

The breathless way she said his name made him molten hot.

"Not…too…much?" His voice was as rough as cold asphalt.

She shifted beneath him and every wiggle steamed a few brain cells. "Just right."

His control wavered. He withdrew and eased in again and again, faster each time. He tried to keep from thrusting too deep, too hard, but when she linked her ankles at the base of his spine he lost it. Instinct took over. Her nails scored his back, his butt, his chest. Her teeth nipped his lip, his shoulder, his neck. He told himself he couldn't be hurting her because she met each thrust and countered each swivel of his hips, and the sexy-as-hell noises coming from her mouth were signs of pleasure not pain.

He buried his face in her neck and quit fighting. The fire rushed from his toes and his fingertips to coalesce in his gut and consume him as his climax roasted him alive. "I'm coming, baby."

Her cry and the squeeze and release of her body told him she was with him. After the last spasm of pleasure faded, his muscles went lax. He caught himself before he crushed her. Braced on his elbows, he battled to regulate his breathing.

As the smoke slowly cleared from his skull he told himself that great sex was all they'd shared. Nothing more. It didn't matter that whatever he and Nicole had just done beat the hell out of anything he'd ever done before. He wouldn't be stupid enough to fall for another woman who could screw him over the way his ex had or the way his mother had his father.

Women were fickle and they fought dirty.

He needed to remember his relationship with Nicole was a short-term alliance. She had a product he wanted and a service he needed. If they had a pleasant interval in the process, so be it. But it would be temporary.

But as his lids grew heavy and his muscles turned to lead he decided making love with her had been a big mistake. Sex clouded the issues. But even as he acknowledged the mistake, he knew he'd repeat it. How could he not?

But he was strong enough to keep his priorities straight. He'd keep his eye on the job of getting custody of his child and never forget for one moment to look out for number one.

Ten

They hadn't used protection.

Every lax, sated muscle in Nicole's body went rigid.

What's going to happen? You're already pregnant with his child, and you know from his medical records that he doesn't have anything contagious.

Still…

She had never been careless. Never. She didn't have sex often, and when she did she didn't forget to protect herself. Physically or emotionally. Tonight she'd forgotten both.

Why had she chosen to drop her usual caution with Ryan? She eased onto her side in his bed and studied him in the dim light. His face had relaxed in sleep, softening his lips and the grooves beside his mouth. His hair was a spiky wreck from her fingers grabbing fistfuls of the thick strands. The sheet he'd pulled over them barely covered his privates.

Ohmigod. Were those scratch marks on his shoulders?

A wave of embarrassment burned over her. She'd never marked a lover before. She wasn't the type to lose control to that extent. Or she hadn't been until tonight when she'd been careless and out of control.

Just like your mother.

Alarms shrieked in her subconscious.

She had to get out of here.

She didn't want to talk to Ryan or look him in the eye until she figured out why she'd let herself go. She'd read that some women were more sensitive during pregnancy and more easily aroused. If her multiple orgasms were an indicator, she must be one of them. That had to be it. She had a case of raging pregnancy hormones, a body primed for sex, and he was her only outlet.

Are you sure it's not more than that?

It couldn't be. She and Ryan barely knew each other.

So he'd guessed she needed to de-stress after the ultrasound. Big deal. And so what if he'd realized she had a headache before she'd admitted it to herself. They had nothing in common except their baby, chemistry and a shared past of acting out to get their parents' attention. None of that meant anything. Or did it?

Was this the connection she'd always yearned for?

Couldn't be.

Her feelings for him were definitely…intense. She'd never experienced anything as powerful as what she and Ryan had shared with anyone—not even Patrick, the only man she'd ever loved and ever would love.

But she wasn't in love with Ryan. Love was soft and cuddly like a cozy fleece blanket. Her feelings for Ryan were more like coarse wool. Rough, prickly and uncomfortable.

Except making love with him had been… *amazing.*

Uneasiness wrapped around her like a spider-web. She needed to go.

Holding her breath and trying not to shake the mattress, she inched out from under the sheet. When her feet touched the rug she exhaled in relief and then took another deep breath before carefully levering herself off the bed. She didn't breathe again until she had both feet on the floor.

She checked to make sure his eyes were still closed. The steady rise and fall of his bare chest caught her attention. The man was built like a gold medal swimmer, all defined muscles, wide shoulders and sleek bronzed skin. Just looking at him raised her temperature.

Get out before he wakes.

She scooped up her panties, shoes and dress and tiptoed out of his bedroom. She didn't stop moving until she reached a puddle of moonlight in his living room where she pulled on her clothes. The loud rustling of her dress made her wince and look over her shoulder for signs of motion in the bed. None. She struggled with the zipper but managed to get it only halfway up.

Carrying her shoes, she headed for the door. *Her purse.* Cringing, she stopped. Where had she left it? And then remembered Ryan had slipped her tiny clutch into the pocket of his tux jacket at the gala. She couldn't leave without it since her cash, credit card, house key and cell phone were inside.

Argh. She couldn't even call Lea to come and get her unless she used Ryan's phone or the one at the gatehouse. Even if she could call Lea, she wouldn't. How could she explain the situation to her friend when she didn't understand it herself? And Lea would demand an explanation.

Nicole raked her fingers through her tangled hair. Why had she slept with Ryan? Wasn't their relationship complicated enough without throwing an affair into the mix?

But it had seemed like a good idea at the time. She'd been rattled by Beth's obvious avoidance and her family's lack of a bond and she'd needed someone. Someone who understood her situation. She'd been carried away by the romance of the evening and turned on by dancing close to him. Falling into bed with him had made sense. Then. Now it felt more like she'd slept with the enemy—the one man who could cost her everything that mattered to her.

She eyed the exit and then his bedroom doorway, torn between the bad choice of calling Lea from the guardhouse for rescue and the worse one of staying. Dismay settled over her like a wet blanket. She had to go back into Ryan's bedroom to retrieve her purse.

She deposited her shoes on an end table and tiptoed back into the room. Her dress *swished* with each step, the sound echoing off the hard surfaces of his apartment. She paused just inside the threshold and scanned the space around the bed. Trying to locate his black coat in a dark room challenged her especially since his decor was all black. Black bed, comforter, sheets and even a black rug on the dark charcoal slate floor.

Where had he thrown his jacket? She spotted it draped across the corner of the bench at the end of the bed and took one careful step and then another toward it.

"Going somewhere?" Ryan's husky voice asked.

Nicole nearly jumped out of her skin. "I need my purse."

"Were you sneaking out on me?" he asked, his voice laced with disbelief as he sat up in bed and turned on a lamp.

Heat rushed her face. She ducked her chin, smoothed her hair then reached for his jacket. "I was going to let you sleep."

"I'll drive you home." He tossed off the sheet and rose from the bed, all lean muscles and masculine vitality.

She couldn't stop herself from soaking him up any more than she could stop a Boeing Business Jet bare-handed. The desire she'd thought quenched rekindled deep inside her.

"I appreciate the offer, but it's not necessary. I'll call a cab."

With his eyes locked on hers, he strolled toward her, setting her heart thumping double-time. He halted inches away, plucked his coat from her hands and tossed it on the bed out of her reach. He dragged his knuckles down her arm, raking up a trail of goose bumps. "I brought you. I'll take you home."

A tingle of unease danced over her skin. If she could react this strongly to Ryan, what did that say about her feelings for Patrick? The question rattled her. She didn't have an answer. She needed privacy to figure this out. A long hot bath…a glass of wine… No. No wine.

A very old memory seeped into her brain of her mother playing a song over and over. "Torn Between Two Lovers." Nicole couldn't have been more than five. And now she was living that life. Was she repeating her mother's mistakes?

"I—I need to go."

Ryan picked up his pants and stepped into them, pulling them over his bare buttocks. Next he reached for his shirt. Watching him put it back on was equally as heart-accelerating as watching him remove it had been. She did not need to find him any more appealing than she already did, but her palms-damp, lips-dry reaction couldn't be denied.

Pressing a cold hand to her hot chest, she turned her back. Ryan's fingers nudged her spine. She jumped and arousal shivered over her. He pulled up her zipper.

Pregnancy hormones. That's all this is.

Or was it? At the moment she wasn't sure of anything.

Nicole awoke Saturday morning determined to make a decision one way or the other. Living in limbo was tearing her apart.

Was this her baby? Or was it Beth's?

She had to move forward and that meant confronting her sister. She lifted a hand and knocked on her sister's front door instead of walking in the way she usually did. Patrick opened the door. Surprise stole her breath. She hadn't expected to run into him. He always shot eighteen holes with his coworkers on Saturday mornings.

He looked about as happy to see her as she was to see him—which was not at all. A first for her. She blamed her strange reaction on not being ready to face him when she'd washed off Ryan's scent only a few hours ago.

She swallowed to ease her dry mouth. "Hi. Aren't you playing golf today?"

"No." The corners of Patrick's mouth had a

downward, dissatisfied turn. Had he always frowned like that?

She tried to recall, but the only face in her mind was Ryan's, particularly, Ryan's face just before he'd left her at her door last night after a devastating good-night kiss. The intensity of her reciprocal need had frightened her. She'd almost invited him in.

"I need to talk to Beth."

"She's making an early-morning grocery run."

He hesitated and shifted on his bare feet. She felt as if she were seeing him for the first time. He wasn't as tall as she remembered, and his sandy-blond hair looked washed out. Wait. Were those gray roots? Had he been coloring his hair?

"Do you want to come in and wait?"

Not the most gracious invitation she'd ever heard, but what choice did she have when Beth refused to return her calls? "Yes. Thanks."

"Coffee?"

She wished she could. She probably hadn't slept more than two hours after Ryan left her. How could she sleep with her body humming and her mind churning? Not even a warm bath had helped. Her life had gone from smooth flying to extreme turbulence seemingly overnight. "I can't. I've cut out caffeine. But thanks."

"Right. So…" An awkward silence stretched between them.

Until now she'd always been comfortable with Patrick, despite him dumping her, because she'd made a tremendous effort to keep things friendly. She hadn't wanted either him or Beth to know how much his change of heart had hurt her. After all, when she'd brought him home to meet her family no words of love or promises of forever had been spoken between them.

She focused on the reason she'd come. "Patrick, do you and Beth still want to adopt my baby?"

He looked away and gulped his coffee. "A baby is all Beth wants. The only reason she keeps me around is for my sperm."

Nicole winced. Ryan was right. There was definitely trouble in paradise—trouble a baby might not fix. "I'm sure that's not true."

He eyed her with a combination of incredulity and pity. "You don't know your sister at all. You only see what she wants you to see. Beth never does anything that doesn't benefit Beth."

That didn't sound good. "Maybe the two of you should see a marriage counselor."

"For that to work she'd have to admit she might be wrong. That's not going to happen."

True. Beth was a perfectionist. If she couldn't do something right then she'd prefer not to do it at all.

The look in his eyes turned downright ugly. "You were with him last night. You left with him."

His accusatory tone raised a red flag. She hoped her cheeks weren't as flushed as they felt. "Ryan? We rode together."

"He just wants his kid. He doesn't want you."

The cruel words stabbed deeply, and as Patrick stared at her she realized she'd never seen him look this unattractive.

"You don't know that, Patrick." But was he right? Was the baby the only reason Ryan had slept with her? No. His desire had been too strong, too real.

"You were always the smarter sister. Don't be stupid over this guy."

A compliment followed by bitter, petty words.

This was not the man she'd fallen in love with in college. She took a mental step back and reminded herself of the stress Patrick had been under. The visit was not going the way she'd anticipated, and she didn't like the side her former lover was showing. She had to get her answers and get out of here.

"Patrick, could you love a child that isn't yours?"

His lips twisted into a petulant line as he stared into his mug. "It's Beth's decision."

Not the enthusiastic reply she'd wanted. "That's not an answer."

"It's the only one you're going to get from me."

Nicole had a sinking feeling that whatever Beth decided Patrick would not welcome her baby with open arms. Could she blame him for not wanting to raise another man's child? Some people handled adoption beautifully. They accepted and loved the gift they were given. But some didn't.

Now that she thought about it, Patrick had always been possessive and particular about *his* things. When they'd been dating he'd never even let her drive his car although he'd driven hers often enough. He'd never shared his dessert or even let her sip from his drink. What was his, was *his.* How had she missed his selfish streak?

"I should have married you," he grumbled.

Nicole couldn't breathe. Those were the words she'd been waiting to hear for a very long time, but they didn't give her the satisfaction she'd expected. Instead, they repulsed her. How could he say or think that now? How could he do that to Beth? His family would be ashamed to hear him speak that way.

How could you have believed you loved him all these years? He's a jerk.

Sadness weighted her chest as the understanding dawned. She had been so afraid of behaving like her mother that she'd convinced herself she could only love one man in her lifetime, and she'd chosen the wrong man for the wrong reasons. She hadn't loved Patrick. She'd fallen for his family—the kind of family she'd always craved. The kind of family she wanted for her baby if she couldn't have it herself.

A hollow ache filled her belly. "When is Beth due back?"

Patrick cocked his head at the sound of a car in the driveway. "That's probably her."

He turned on his heel and stalked out of the kitchen. Seconds later she heard his feet stomping upstairs.

As much as Nicole dreaded the conversation to come, she had to get it over with. She met Beth in the garage. "Hi. Need help with the groceries?"

"It's just one bag."

Uneasiness swirled in Nicole's belly. "Can we talk?"

"I have to get ready for a lunch appointment."

Nicole had always put her family first, but it was time she put herself and her baby at the top of the list. "Beth, I need five minutes."

"Make it quick," Beth grumbled grudgingly. Nicole followed her inside. Beth went straight for the coffeepot. "What is it?"

"The baby isn't biologically yours or Patrick's. I will understand if you don't want to stick with our agreement. Just please, be honest with me. Tell me what you want."

"I don't want to have this conversation."

"It's overdue. Beth, this is not a good time for

you and Patrick to add to the strain your marriage is already under with a baby. You need to focus on the two of you."

"My marriage is none of your business."

The caustic words hurt. Nicole tried a different tactic. "I don't think Patrick can love this baby."

"Patrick can't love anyone but Patrick." Beth's bitterness rang loud and clear.

Living with two parents who said ugly things about each other would not be a healthy environment for a child. Nicole wet her lips and took a deep breath. She swallowed the lump in her throat and rubbed her agitated stomach. *Say it.* "I want to keep my baby."

Beth drew herself up, her face indignant and flushed with angry color. She slammed her mug on the counter, sloshing the dark brew over the rim. "You'd betray me after all I've done for you? You never intended to go through with the adoption, did you?"

Regret settled heavily on Nicole's shoulders. "Of course I did, and I still would if I thought it was the right thing to do. But it's not. Once Ryan came on the scene you and Patrick lost interest.

And who could blame you? It's not your husband's child. Beth, you avoid me. You don't return my phone calls or even my e-mails."

"I didn't call you because I couldn't stand to see you get everything I wanted once again."

Shock rocked Nicole to the soles of her shoes. "What are you talking about?"

"Everything always came easy for you, Nicole. Boyfriends. Good grades. College. Life. You even got pregnant on the first try. I had to work for everything, and I still got left on the sidelines."

She'd had no idea Beth harbored such resentment. "You chose to be on the sidelines, Beth. You like playing it safe."

As soon as Nicole said the words, she knew they were true. Why hadn't she noticed before that Beth liked to watch life rather than live it?

"Well, this time I win. I'm pregnant, too. And I don't need your damned baby to have a family. I'm having three of my own. Mine and Patrick's. Three! Top that."

Nicole staggered back not only at the news but also at Beth's over-the-top competitive and emotional response. "You're pregnant? How?"

"I've been seeing a specialist in New York for months. That's why I've missed work. He confirmed last week that I'm carrying triplets. We thought I might be pregnant before the Labor Day picnic, but we weren't sure."

"Congratulations," Nicole uttered automatically. Part of her was thrilled that her sister's dream of having a family was coming true. But another part resented Beth for putting her through this emotional wringer while she continued to try to conceive. It felt like a betrayal.

Anger licked through her. "What was I? Your insurance policy? You'd keep my baby only if you didn't conceive your own? What if the fertility clinic hadn't made a mistake? What if this had been Patrick's child?"

"Then you'd have what you've wanted all along—a piece of my husband."

Nicole recoiled. "I have never made one inappropriate move toward Patrick."

"But you wanted to. You loved him first. But don't forget, you've signed over your rights to the baby you're carrying. You can't keep it."

"You're pregnant with triplets! Why would you want my baby, too?"

"Because we need the money Ryan offered. The fertility treatments were expensive. And there will be even more money from the malpractice suit we're filing against the fertility clinic for their screwup."

Nicole stumbled backward. For a fraction of a second she hated both Beth and Patrick. She had offered them a gift that would have torn out her heart, and they were using her with no regard for her feelings whatsoever.

She reined in her anger. "Don't plan on using my baby or me as your cash cow. If I have to liquidate everything I own and take out loans to pay the legal fees, I will make absolutely certain you don't see a dime from my baby. And Ryan will side with me."

"The law is on my side. That contract is as ironclad as it can possibly be." A disgusted sound rumbled from Beth's throat. "Look at yourself, Nicole. You've become our mother."

She flinched. "What is that supposed to mean?"

"You've fallen for your lover and you think

just because you're knocked up with his brat he'll marry you. Well, your Ryan is going to turn out just like Lauren's father. He's going to use you and toss you aside."

"You don't know that's what happened to our mother."

"Yes, I do. My bedroom was next to Mom and Dad's. I heard their arguments. Everybody knows they didn't love each other, that Dad married her for her money to keep Hightower Aviation afloat. What you don't know is that she fell in love with Lauren's father. But she got dumped and so will you. Once Ryan gets his hands on this kid you will be nothing to him. He'll cut you off, and you'll be lucky if you ever get to see your baby again."

Horrified, Nicole braced herself on the counter. "You're wrong."

Beth's laugh held no humor. "We'll see, won't we?"

Nicole broke out in a cold sweat. She had to talk to Ryan. He was the only one who could help her now. With the echoes of Beth's prediction ringing in her ears, she fled to her car and raced toward Ryan's condo.

Her stomach twisted with anxiety but a new realization seeped into her conscience. If she didn't love Patrick, then that left the door open for loving someone else—someone who made her feel more alive than she ever had before.

Someone who obviously wanted a family as badly as she did.

Someone who might help her keep her baby.

Ryan.

Eleven

"I need your help," Nicole blurted the second Ryan opened the door to his condo Saturday afternoon.

He took in her subtle curves outlined by a lavender cashmere cowl-neck sweater and navy slacks and hunger licked through him. He hadn't been able to get Friday night out of his head. The way she looked. The way she tasted. The way she'd shuddered in his arms and clenched him in her slick body.

The way she'd trusted him, and the guilt he'd felt after dropping her off.

The tension straining her pale face told him they wouldn't be revisiting his bed in the next few minutes for more of that stellar sex. Just as well. His conscience was giving him hell.

Even though he'd known it would be a mistake, he'd come close to asking her to stay all night. Dangerous territory. How many times had he seen a friend start thinking with his dick and lose his common sense? The only thing worse was getting emotionally involved. That left a man weak and at the whims of the woman pulling his strings.

It wasn't going to happen to him. He'd keep his eye on the goal.

But damn, the sex had been great, their chemistry unbelievable. He wanted more. But sex and the baby they shared were her only appeal. And once he had his kid, he wouldn't need Nicole. For now he needed to pull his head together and get back in the game.

He stepped away from the door. "Come in."

Nicole headed straight for his den, her sexy high-heeled boots rapping out a rhythm on his slate floors. She stopped abruptly short of the windows and turned. Her fear of heights shouldn't be endearing, but it was. Probably because she fought so hard to hide it. But the telling way she backed away from his window each time she got too near the glass gave her away.

Her bottom lip was swollen as if she'd been biting it. "I'm sorry I didn't call, but I didn't have your home or cell number."

He dug his wallet out of his pants as he followed her into the room, withdrew a business card, located a pen and wrote his personal numbers on the back. He offered the information to her. "Now you have all my numbers."

She took the card and the touch of her fingertips against his zapped him with an electric charge. Static, no doubt. Or maybe just lust.

She shoved the info into her pocket without looking at it. "Beth is pregnant with triplets."

That should have been good news, but even though she hid it well, he could feel Nicole's anxiety rolling off her in waves. Odd. He'd never been that sensitive to another woman's emotions. "I thought she couldn't get pregnant."

"She's been seeing a new fertility specialist behind my back."

"She and Patrick should be willing to cancel the surrogacy contract now." That put him head-to-head with Nicole, who'd already relinquished her parental rights. His odds of winning looked good. But the pain and panic in her eyes tugged at him. His winning meant her losing.

"You would think so, but she intends to hold me to it."

"Why would she if she's pregnant?"

"She wants the money you offered to defray the cost of her medical expenses. And she plans to sue the clinic for malpractice and make even more money."

The strength of his anger on Nicole's behalf surprised him. He rocked back on his heels. The greedy bastards. Nicole was willing to cut out her heart for them, and they were going to squeeze out every last cent at her expense.

And how is what you're doing any better? You're pitting her against her sister.

He ignored the pesky protest of his conscience. "That doesn't surprise me."

"Ryan…" Nicole's gaze dropped to the floor

and her hands fisted. She took a deep breath as if gathering her courage, and then lifted her eyes again. "I'm going to try and revoke my surrogacy contract. My attorney says it's almost impossible, but as you said, Beth and Patrick are not good candidates for parenting our baby. Their marriage is in trouble. Add in her high-risk multiple pregnancy, and I think I stand at least a slim chance of succeeding. And then…we'll share custody. You and me."

His heart kicked faster. Dissension among the Hightowers had been his plan all along. It brought his goal of having a child to cinch his position at Patrick Architectural closer. But sharing custody wasn't an option.

His relationship with Nicole would be a casualty, but a long-term or permanent involvement with her had never been part of his plan. All that mattered was keeping his father from selling the company out from under him. He had to win. And for him to win somebody had to lose.

Success had never felt so lousy.

"I'll speak to my attorney." But he wouldn't be

initiating the proceedings Nicole expected. He'd be doing what he did best. Looking out for number one. The only person who never let him down.

Beth stormed into Nicole's office late Monday afternoon and hurled a sheaf of papers across her desk. "I told you the bastard would screw you over. And he's taking us down with you."

Nicole reached for the scattered sheets. "What are you talking about?"

"He's trying to steal our baby."

"He who?" But she knew. Tension spiraled up her spine.

"Ryan Patrick."

The letterhead from one of Knoxville's most powerful and prestigious attorneys caught Nicole's attention. She scanned the text and ice seeped into her veins. Her arms went weak and the document slipped from her grasp. "Ryan is suing for sole custody of my baby."

"*My* baby. You promised this baby to me."

"And you don't want it. You plan to sell it like a black-market baby."

"I'm not going to sell it. I'm agreeing to settle

custody out of court. The money was Ryan's idea. Remember? He came to us."

"Same difference, Beth. You're taking money for a child that isn't even yours—one I will carry and nourish and love for nine months. A baby I ache for. And you intend to rip it from my arms for money."

"You agreed to this."

"I agreed to give you and Patrick the family you so desperately wanted because it would make you happy. Now all I ask is that you be as unselfish for me."

"I've done nothing but give to you my entire life. I gave up dates to babysit you."

"We had nannies who were paid to do that."

"I was there for you. I gave you my time, my attention and my advice when our mother wouldn't give you hers," Beth continued in a righteous tone.

"And now you're taking what matters most. My child."

Beth emitted a furious hiss and stormed out of the office. Nicole let her go. She tried to gather her shattered composure and focus on the issue.

She wanted to believe Ryan wasn't betraying her. Maybe he had a strategy—one that would get around the surrogacy contract she'd signed.

She rose on shaky legs and crossed to the fax machine. Within moments the pages were on their way to her attorney. Then Nicole returned to her desk and dug Ryan's business card from her purse. She had to talk to him. She punched in his office number.

"Nicole Hightower for Ryan Patrick, please," she said as soon as the receptionist answered.

"He's unavailable at the moment, Ms. Hightower. May I take a message?"

She needed him now. "No. Thank you."

She dialed his cell number. Voice mail picked up. "It's Nicole. Please call me."

She tried his house and left another message. Where was he? Was he refusing to answer because he saw her name on caller ID? Why would he avoid her unless he had something to hide? A sick feeling invaded her stomach. What if Beth was right? What if Ryan had used her to weaken Beth and Patrick's claim on the baby?

She had to find him. She bolted to her feet and

raced out, barely pausing by Lea's desk. "I have to leave early."

She didn't give her assistant a chance to ask questions. Within minutes she was in her car and headed toward the glass office tower housing Patrick Architectural. She hustled inside. The elevator rocketed upward.

She stormed into the thirtieth-floor offices just before five o'clock and marched up to the receptionist's desk. "I need to see Ryan Patrick. It's urgent."

The woman took her name, called someone on the phone and then pointed. "Last door on the right."

Fear and apprehension made Nicole tremble as she made her way across the plush carpet. The door was open. An older lady rose from behind a maple desk. "Ryan will see you now."

She gestured for Nicole to go through another door. Ryan stood by a drafting table in the corner of the room. Nicole quickly scanned his office. The frosted glass, maple and chrome furnishings were just as modern as the decor of his house. But whereas his home was all dark colors, straight lines and sharp corners, his office was brightly lit and decorated in pale neutrals with furniture comprised of curves and round-edged, frosted glass.

He laid down his tools and turned. The carefully blank expression on his face made her stomach sink. “I take it you’ve heard from Beth.”

She met his solemn gaze. “Please tell me you have a master strategy that will allow me to co-parent my child with you. Because the petition doesn’t read that way.”

Ryan’s jaw went rigid. “I’m sorry, Nicole. I’m suing for full custody.”

A crushing sensation settled in her chest. “What about me?”

“You relinquished your rights. The waiver you signed is airtight.”

She wound her arms around her middle. “Ryan, this is my baby.”

“I don’t have time for a lengthy custody battle. I need a child now.”

“Why? Why do you have to do this?”

“My father is planning to retire next year. Like you, he equates fast cars, boats and motorcycles and a bachelor pad with an unwillingness to grow up or think ahead. He's threatening to sell Patrick Architectural out from under me. I hired a surrogate to give him a grandchild to prove I am planning for the future. Instead, I got you."

Horrified, she backed away. Ryan had encouraged her to turn against her sister, most likely irrevocably damaging her family relationship. For greed? "You don't want a baby at all. You just want this company?"

"What I want is to disabuse my father of his old-fashioned notion that a man has to be married to be mature and responsible and dedicated to his job. I'm sorry for the pain this is going to cause you, Nicole. But you're young. You'll have other children."

Her throat tightened. Her heart ached. "Was sleeping with me a way to coerce me into cutting Beth and Patrick out of the picture?"

His hesitation spoke volumes. "We have great sexual chemistry."

Sexual chemistry? Was that all they shared? She'd been telling herself the same thing. So why did it slice like a razor when he said it?

"What you're telling me is that this child was merely a means to an end for you and that you want it for all the wrong reasons. A baby deserves to be loved, Ryan, not just used."

"He became more than a tool when I saw him on the ultrasound."

The pain swelled inside her until she was almost dizzy with it. "I don't believe you."

He strode behind his desk, yanked open the top drawer and pulled something out. With a flick of his wrist he slung the object across the table just like he'd tossed those letters the day they'd met. A twin to the picture he'd given her slid to a stop near the edge in front of her. Then he flipped open his wallet, revealing a smaller version of the same photo.

He shoved his wallet back into his pocket. "Believe that. This is my son or daughter, and I want it as badly as you do. I've been robbed of a child once before. I won't let it happen again."

"That's why I thought you'd understand how much being a part of my child's life means to me. But you used me. Just like you planned to use and discard your surrogate. Ryan, I would never keep you from your child. Why can't we share custody?"

"Shared custody leaves the door open for you to change your mind and use the child as a weapon against me. I won't let that happen."

Head reeling, knees weak, she needed to sit down, but she didn't dare reveal her weakness to the enemy. Beth and Patrick were right. All Ryan wanted was the baby she carried. He'd told her that from day one. So why did it hurt so much to have it verified now?

Because you were falling for him.

Correction. She'd already fallen for him like a climber slipping off the face of a glacier. There would be nothing but pain in her immediate future.

By hiding behind her old feelings for Patrick, she'd fooled herself into believing she couldn't be swept off her feet by Ryan's old-fashioned gestures, the understanding she'd seen in his eyes and the passion his touch ignited. But he'd slipped past her defenses when she'd thought herself safe.

It was like being kicked when she was already down from Beth's treachery. She backed blindly toward the door. "I will see you in court, and I promise I will fight you to my last cent. No child deserves a heartless manipulative bastard like you for a father."

She turned on her heel and fled because if she stayed, she was going to break down in front of him. Ryan's betrayal was ten times worse than Patrick's because, unlike her first love, Ryan knew he was tearing out her heart by taking her baby. But she couldn't bear to lose what was left of her pride by letting him know she'd fallen in love with him.

A heartless manipulative bastard.

The description fit like a cheap shirt.

Ryan wanted to go after Nicole. But what could he say?

She was right. He'd gone into this surrogacy plan with purely selfish motives. He hadn't intended for anyone to get hurt. But there was no denying the agony clouding Nicole's beautiful aqua eyes before she'd left.

His lungs felt tight, but not because he was afraid of her threat to take him to court. The law was on his side, and according to his attorney, Nicole had a slim-to-none chance of getting custody as a result of the waiver she'd signed. He, on the other hand, stood a very good probability of defeating Beth and Patrick who had no DNA connection to the baby whatsoever.

Divide and conquer, his attorney had suggested, and Ryan had done exactly that. But where was the satisfaction he should be feeling? He raked a hand through his hair.

His father entered without knocking. "Was that Nicole I saw getting into the elevator?"

"Yes."

"She looked upset. Is there a problem with the plane or the flight?"

HAMC had scheduled a test run for the Patrick Architectural executives to show the rest of the team how their mobile office worked. "No."

"You left the ball with her Friday night."

"Yes."

"I like her, Ryan. She's the kind of woman you should have been dating all these years instead of your brainless twits."

"Yes."

His father frowned. "What's with the monosyllabic answers? Not your usual style."

Hell, he might as well get it out in the open. Owning up to a mistake was the first step toward fixing it. And he had made a mistake—one that might not be forgivable.

He picked up the photo and offered it to his father. "Nicole is carrying my child. Your grandchild. The one you've been harping about for years."

His father stared at the picture in silence and then his gaze met Ryan's. "So you lied. You were dating her before you suggested the plane."

"No."

"Then what? You had a one-night stand? Didn't I warn you to be careful?"

"I hired a surrogate. The plan backfired."

His father went silent once more then finally said, "Explain."

"I want to be president of Patrick Architectural when you retire. I'm damned good at my job, and I have the awards to prove it. I know this company. I know this business. I shouldn't have to be married, drive a sedan, have a house in the suburbs filled with children or live *your* dream to win your approval.

"Despite the decade of sweat equity I've put in at P.A. you keep demanding more proof that I consider this firm my future. But whatever I do, it's never enough. How can I prove I've never wanted to work anywhere else? I thought a kid, another generation of Patricks to carry on, would demonstrate my…loyalty to the firm."

Hearing his plot out loud made Ryan realize he'd been an idiot. How had he ever considered this a logical plan? "Wrong move. I know that now."

His father stood the frame up on the desk. "Where does Nicole come into this? I don't see her as the type to hire out her body."

"You're right. She's the kind of woman who always puts family first and herself last. The antithesis of my mother and my ex-wife."

His father grimaced. "Your mother demanded a lot of attention. But sometimes no matter how much you give someone it's never enough because the void they're trying to fill is internal. The more your mother tried to use you, the more I backed off because you kept getting hurt. I'm sorry you were caught in the middle of our breakup.

"As for your ex, you did the honorable thing in marrying her. Too bad she had no honor or honesty in her. But that's in the past and it can't be changed. Tell me about the present. What's Nicole's role?"

"Nicole volunteered to carry a child for her infertile sister even though relinquishing the baby would rip her heart out. But the fertility clinic made a mistake and inseminated Nicole with my sperm instead of her brother-in-law's. I'm suing for full custody."

"And the sister's claim?"

"She's pregnant with triplets and no longer needs this child."

His father clamped a hand on his shoulder. "You know I'm old-fashioned, and I won't deny I've made my desire for grandchildren clear, but I pressured you into marrying for the sake of a baby once already. I won't repeat that mistake. But is marriage out of the question? I've seen you two together, son. You and Nicole have something…something that might be worth fighting for."

"I'll never marry again. You know why."

"But is denying the woman her child the right thing to do?"

Before he'd met Nicole, Ryan could have answered in the affirmative without reservations. Now he wasn't so sure. He'd had more candidates for the surrogate position than he'd had time to interview. Women competing for the right to sell their bodies and their babies. But Nicole wasn't like them. "She signed away her rights."

"Circumstances have changed. She's not giving her sister a gift of love anymore."

"This is my child."

"And hers." His father pointed out the obvious. "Is there a reason why you think Nicole would be an unfit mother?"

Guilt stabbed him. "None whatsoever."

"However oddly your relationship began, you've created a child together. If you can't love her, then let her go and work out a solution for the child that allows it to benefit from both parents. But be aware that in the future some other man may be stepfathering your child."

The words hit Ryan like a fist to the gut,

punching the air from his lungs. He hadn't thought about Nicole with another man. A woman like her had too much to offer to be alone for long. But the idea of her in someone else's bed, someone else's arms made him want to crawl out of his skin.

He wasn't feeling territorial, was he? He'd never been possessive of a woman before—not even his ex. But the idea of Nicole crying out as some other man drove into her slender body, of her shuddering as the faceless ass brought her to orgasm, ripped a hole in Ryan's stomach and spilled burning acid through his body.

"I can't risk another marriage."

"Another betrayal, you mean. I understand. We all want to avoid that kind of pain. And some of us never find the courage to try again."

The solemn statement staggered Ryan. Until now his father had never admitted that the divorce had hurt him. He'd hidden his feeling behind a gruff, no-nonsense facade.

"But, Ryan, think long and hard before you deprive a baby of its mother. No one will love the child more. That's why I let you go. It wasn't that

I didn't love you or want you around. It's that you were your mother's life, her reason for being. I'm not sure what would have happened to her if I'd taken you away."

Surprised, he searched his father's face to see if he were telling the truth, and found pain and regret in his father's eyes. "I wish you'd told me that sooner, Dad."

"I didn't want to diminish your love for your mother by pointing out her weaknesses. We all have flaws. It's how we deal with them that counts. And I loved your mother despite hers."

"But you divorced her."

"She divorced me. Your mother was the love of my life. After you came along I wanted to give you both more. A bigger house. Private school. Nicer cars. A Cornell education like your grandfather and I had. I worked extra hours, probably more than I should have. Your mother became convinced I was cheating on her. I wasn't, but she wouldn't believe me, and once the trust is gone…" Sadness deepened the lines on his face.

And Ryan had just destroyed Nicole's trust.

His father shrugged. "Still, I got you out of the

deal, so even though the marriage ended badly, the pain was worth it."

"Dad, I don't want my kid to be caught in a tug-of-war."

"Then you'd better work out a fair solution you and Nicole can live with. Better that than a vicious legal battle that drags on for a decade. But remember, the child's welfare always comes first. *Always.* Even if it might be the most difficult decision you'll ever make. Walking away from you was that for me."

Ryan looked at his father with a new perspective, one that allowed him a clearer view of the decisions his father had made over the years.

And now Ryan was in the same no-win situation. Did he look out for number one the way he always had? Or did he put his child first? And could he ever regain Nicole's trust? Right now that job seemed to be the most urgent.

He stared into blue eyes so similar to the ones he saw in the mirror each morning, but these eyes were older, wiser and more generous. "Dad, this is one time I wish you could tell me what to do."

His father patted his shoulder. "And this is the

one time no one but you has the answer. Whatever you decide, son, I'll back you one hundred percent. But do the right thing by my grandchild."

His father had said it perfectly. No one would love this child more than Nicole. No one had a more generous heart. But granting her joint custody meant leaving the door open for another chunk of his heart to be imploded if she decided later to cut him out of her and their baby's life.

Was the risk worth it?

Twelve

Nicole stood in the boardroom early Tuesday morning staring at her siblings and her parents and listening to the hum of their conversations as she gathered her courage for what she had to do. Only Patrick and Lauren, neither of whom owned any HAMC stock, were missing.

It would be much easier to do as her mother had done and simply disappear. But life on the run really wasn't fair to a child. Besides, her baby deserved to know its aunts, uncles and grandparents even if the Hightowers weren't the warmest, fuzziest bunch. And Ryan had been robbed of a child once already. Nicole couldn't do that to him again. That meant taking the easy way out wasn't an option.

"I'm pregnant."

Her words silenced the chatter. All eyes turned to her.

Beth crossed her arms and stuck her jaw out at a belligerent angle. "Great. Make this all about you again."

Nicole realized Patrick was right. She hadn't known her sister. Otherwise, she would have recognized Beth's petty jealousy long ago.

"Who's the father?" Trent asked in a deadly calm voice.

"Ryan Patrick. That's why I asked to be excused as his CAM." Fist clenched, Trent rose looking ready to do battle. "Sit down, big brother. This situation is far more complicated than you think." He resettled uneasily in his chair.

"Let me begin at the beginning. Beth and Patrick asked me to be a surrogate for them and I agreed. I was supposed to have Patrick's child, but the fertility clinic transposed the first and last names of the donors, and I'm carrying Ryan's baby instead."

Bodies shifted around the table as they digested the information. "In the meantime, congratulations are in order. Beth has been seeing a new fertility specialist, and she and Patrick have just discovered they're expecting triplets. They'll need your support in the coming months. Being pregnant with triplets won't be easy. Neither will caring for them after the delivery."

She rested a hand over the slight swell marking her baby and gave her family time to offer Beth their good wishes while she tried to remember her practiced speech without luck.

The conversation died down and everyone's attention returned to her. "In light of Beth's pregnancy, I've decided to keep my baby, but Beth and Patrick and Ryan are also fighting for custody. The battle is likely to get ugly, and the scandal might make headlines. I don't want to turn Hightower Aviation into a battlefield where we destroy our family by choosing sides. If you'd like me to resign, I will, or I can transfer to one of our foreign operation centers."

Her mother stood and every muscle in Nicole's

body tightened. Surely her mother wouldn't denounce her if she'd meant what she'd said about regretting not being there for her children in the past.

Her mother met her gaze. "Scandals come and go. Hightowers survive them. Nicole, you have my full support. And I would hope Beth and Patrick will be mature enough to stop their nonsense and give theirs, as well. Your generosity is overwhelming, and I am proud to call you my daughter."

Relief weakened Nicole and tears clogged her throat. She grasped the table's edge to stay upright. This wasn't the mother she'd known for the past twenty-eight years. "Thank you, Mom."

Beth looked none-too-happy with their mother's pronouncement. "Even if Patrick and I drop the custody battle, Ryan has a damned good chance of winning. He has a DNA link to the baby. And Nicole waived her parental rights."

Jacqueline Hightower looked down her nose at her oldest daughter. "That is my grandbaby Nicole is carrying, and Ryan Patrick has no idea how dangerous a pissed off Hightower can be."

Trent sat forward in his chair. “We’ll go after him with both barrels, Nicole.”

Nicole’s vision blurred and tears burned hot trails on her cheeks. She might lose her baby, but she wouldn’t have to go through it alone. She’d have her family beside her. And while she’d always wanted the Hightowers to be closer, this wasn’t exactly what she had in mind.

“Flowers for you,” Lea said from Nicole’s doorway late Monday afternoon.

Nicole looked up. A large arrangement of mixed blooms in shades of peach, cream, orange and yellow completely obscured her assistant’s torso. “They’re beautiful.”

Lea set them on the corner of Nicole’s desk and turned to go without her usual fifty questions. That was odd, but Nicole let it go. Lea had been tiptoeing cautiously since Nicole had given her the full story two weeks ago.

The sweet fragrance of the blooms filled Nicole’s nose as she searched for a card. Who had sent them and why? It wasn’t her birthday. She hadn’t done anything to warrant an extravagant thank-you from a client. Nor was she the type of woman who regularly—if ever—received flowers from an admirer.

Perhaps Beth had sent them as an apology?

She couldn't find the card. "Lea, did you take the card?"

"I have it."

Ryan's deep voice brought her head up with a jerk. Her stomach and pulse fluttered wildly. She hadn't heard from him in two weeks, but that didn't mean he hadn't been constantly in her thoughts.

He strolled in wearing a black suit, pale yellow shirt and another one of his geometric print ties, this one in greens, blacks and yellows. The man liked his lines which was not surprising since he drew buildings for a living. The small white envelope he held between his fingertips explained why Lea hadn't been pawing through the blooms. She'd known who had the card.

Nicole folded her arms. "My lawyer says I'm not supposed to talk to you."

The slow, sensual way Ryan's intense blue gaze rolled over her reminded her of the night in his bedroom. Beneath her conservative navy suit her skin flushed and dampened. She sank back into her chair, exhaling in a futile attempt to ease her tension.

"Then you must not have talked to her today." He shut her office door, enclosing them in a mouth-drying intimacy. She wasn't ready for this.

"What do you mean?"

"Your sister and brother-in-law have dropped their custody suit. This is between you and me now." He offered the card.

Nicole reluctantly accepted it. She hadn't liked anything he'd given her to read thus far. She slipped the seal and pulled out the plain white folded square. A brass key fell out and clattered onto her desk.

Your new address, he'd written in bold script, followed by a Knoxville street address.

She searched his serious face. "What does this mean?"

"You claimed the house was perfect for raising a family. I bought it. For you."

She shook her head. "Me? I don't understand."

"We both want what's best for our child. I want you to raise our baby in that house."

Raise our baby in that house. Her heart thumped harder. This sounded too good to be true. She must have misunderstood. “I still don’t understand. Why are you doing this, Ryan? What’s in it for you?”

“No one will love our child more than you. Consider custody and the house my gifts to the baby. To both of you. The deed will be in your name as soon as you sign the papers.”

He circled her desk and leaned forward to plant his hands on the arms of her chair, trapping her with his body and those mesmerizing blue eyes. He bent his elbows until his face was level with hers.

Nicole tilted back her head. Her mouth watered. She dampened her lips, wanting his kiss. How could she still want him after what he’d done? And did she dare trust him? Was this a trick? It had to be.

His eyes tracked the sweep of her tongue, but he didn’t move any closer. “There’s a catch.”

Her brain slowly caught gear and shifted forward. Of course there was a catch. “What kind of catch?”

“I want to live there with you.”

He wanted to live with her? She shot backward, rolling the chair out of his reach and bolted to her feet. Pain and disappointment vied for supremacy. "Is this another sneaky, underhanded way to get your father to leave you Patrick Architectural? How low will you go, Ryan?"

He clenched his fists by his sides. "I screwed up. I had tunnel vision. My father has been nagging me for grandchildren for years. I decided to give him exactly what he asked for. I saw the brass ring and nothing more.

"After my ex-wife's betrayal I swore I'd never let anyone or anything matter that much again. But I was wrong. I'd never met anyone like you, Nicole. Someone who always put others first. Someone who gave even though it ripped her heart out. I didn't trust it. I didn't trust you. Now I do."

He stepped closer. She backed up.

"You're always doing for others. When was the last time someone did something for you?"

She put the chair between them. "Taking care of others is my job."

"That's professionally. I meant personally."

"I can take care of my needs."

"Then it's about time someone spoiled you. Let me be that someone. Teach me how."

She didn't dare believe that tender look in his eyes. It had to be fake, another go at hoodwinking her. "Ryan, what are you trying to pull?"

He extracted a thick business-size envelope from his jacket and she rolled her eyes. Déjà vu. The return address from her attorney's office caught her eye. "I asked Meredith Jones to let me deliver this personally."

Her attorney would never have trusted him with anything that could hurt her. Nicole snatched the envelope from his hand and ripped it open. She recognized Meredith's handwriting on the short notepaper clipped to a thick sheaf of papers.

Nicole,
I'll go over the legalese with you later, but the gist is, Ryan Patrick has signed papers granting you sole custody of the baby you carry. He's waived all parental rights if, but only if, *you* raise the child. He would like visitation, but is not forcing the issue.

Details later, but this is legit.
Congratulations, Mommy.
Meredith

Mommy. Nicole clutched the papers to her chest and searched Ryan's face. "What about Patrick Architectural?"

He shrugged. "I'm damned good at what I do. If my father chooses to sell P.A., then I'll move on. I can join another firm or open my own."

"Why, Ryan? Why walk away from something that matters so much to you?"

He inhaled then exhaled slowly. "Because your generosity blows me away. You're the only woman I've ever met who never asked 'What's in it for me?' I've fallen in love with you, Nicole."

Her heart stuttered then lurched into a wild rhythm. She was afraid to believe the emotion thickening his voice and the love she saw in his eyes. She couldn't handle getting her heart broken again.

Her lips quivered. "Don't try to manipulate me with lies."

He flinched. A nerve in his jaw twitched. "I

deserve that. But I have never lied to you except by omission. The passion we shared was real. I know I hurt you. I'd like the chance to make it right. I'm hoping you'll eventually find room in that generous heart of yours for me."

He pushed the chair aside and dropped to one knee. "I want to marry you, Nicole, raise a family with you and spoil you like you've never allowed anyone else to do. But mostly, I want the chance to love you. And I want you to teach me how to be as giving as you are."

She couldn't speak. She ached so badly for what he said to be true. When the silence stretched between them he paled, bowed his head. A few seconds later he nodded and rose stiffly.

"The house and baby are yours. No strings attached. I would like to be as involved in your life and our child's as you'll let me. But if you can't handle that, I'll accept your decision and keep my distance."

He turned and strode toward the door, and it was as if he'd taken her heart and all the oxygen in the room with him as he walked away. She'd never felt so empty. She hadn't hurt this much when she'd realized she'd lost Patrick. Like she couldn't breathe. Like her legs wouldn't support her. Like her world would end without him in it.

This body-consuming craving, the necessity to keep him close was love.

What she'd felt for Patrick had been a tepid imitation. And loving more than once didn't make her weak, like she'd always thought her mother to be. Love gave her the strength to try again until she got it right. And this time she had the right man. Ryan. If she didn't let him get away.

"Ryan, don't go."

He stopped with his hand on the doorknob and slowly pivoted. His face looked drawn and composed, as if he'd donned a mask. But hope flickered in his eyes, and it was that trace of emotion he couldn't hide that told her he wasn't lying about loving her and not just their child.

"I want everything you said. With you. Only you. I love you. And I want to raise this baby—*our* baby—with you."

Love softened his entire face and his tender smile made her eyes burn with happy tears. He quickly closed the distance between them and swept her into his arms and off her feet. He buried his face in her neck and hugged her with almost rib-cracking strength as if he never wanted to let her go.

He drew back, met her gaze and slowly eased her back onto her feet. "On one condition."

She stiffened.

"You start putting yourself first for a change, because you're the one who matters the most to me."

"I'll see what I can do, but I might need your help fulfilling that request."

* * * * *